A
NOBLE
VOID

Matthias Meyer

A
NOBLE
VOID

Matthias Meyer

TEXTEM VERLAG

Was die Stimme
nicht sieht

Katha Schulte

1. Die Stimme

»The voice is in the air.«
(Michel Chion, 1982)

Im Tonfilmkino erscheinen üblicherweise die
Bestandteile Bild und Ton wie aus einem Guss,
von Natur aus zusammengehörig, wobei der Ton
als folgsamer Schatten des Bildes wahrgenom-
men wird. Da synchrone Töne im Unterschied zu
Voiceover- und Musiktönen von ihrem jeweiligen
Bild unmittelbar absorbiert werden, erscheinen
sie zu Unrecht als redundante Information. Dass
der Anschein einer größtmöglichen – allenfalls
überlebensgroßen – Natürlichkeit unter Aufwand
aller zu Gebot stehenden Tricks zu erzeugen ist,
gehört ebenso zum Spiel, wie dass man dem Ton
die Mühe, die er macht, nicht anmerkt. Er gilt
als umso gelungener, je weniger dieser Einsatz
spürbar ist.

Der Komponist und Filmemacher Michel
Chion, Mitarbeiter der *Cahiers du cinéma* und
Verfasser einiger bedeutender Monographien
zum Sound im Kino, betont demgegenüber die
Arbitrarität von Bild und Ton.

Robert Bresson hat die jeweiligen Zusammen-
künfte von Bild und Ton im Film mit Zufallsbe-
kanntschaften verglichen; Michel Chion erfasst in
»Audio-Vision« systematisch die Umstände, unter
denen diese Bekanntschaft im Lauf der Kinogeschichte geschlossen wurde.[1] Das Auditive und
das Visuelle, die beiden Wahrnehmungsmodi
der Audio-Vision beeinflussen einander, nicht in
Harmonie, sondern in einem Vertrag der Wechsel-
seitigkeit. Besondere Bedeutung kommt dabei
der Stimme zu, die im Tonfilm zentral ist.[2] Die
Geschichte des Kinos liest sich unter diesem
Vorzeichen als Geschichte des Zueinanderstre-
bens von Bild und Ton. Der Stummfilm kann
demgegenüber einer Zeit der Unschuld zugerech-
net werden, noch unberührt von der Spaltkraft
der Sprache. Die Vormacht des Sichtbaren geht
sodann mit der gleichzeitigen Abwertung aller
anderen Sinne einher – *sight rules*. Der Sound zieht
sich daraufhin in den Schatten zurück, schreibt
Walter Murch, Bild- und Toneditor von Filmen
wie *The Conversation* und *Apocalypse Now*, im
Vorwort zu »Audio-Vision«.[3]

Die Nachträglichkeit, mit welcher der Ton
zum Filmbild hinzutrat, steht in bezeichnender

Gegenläufigkeit zur Geschichte des Einzelmenschen, der aus dem pränatalen Soundkontinuum, aus dem Dunkel kommend mit der Geburt in die Welt des Sichtbaren eintritt. Umgekehrt hat das Kino, so Murch, seine Jugend, 1892–1927, in einem Spiegelsaal voll stimmloser Bilder verbracht. Dass dem Filmton mehr zuteil würde als eine vorübergehende Phase des Experiments, war nicht vorauszusehen. So beschreibt ein früher Zuschauer den Tonfilm 1929 mit deutlichem Missvergnügen als eine ›seltsame Komödie, bei der die Schauspieler die Texte mit ihren Lippen abformen, während ein geheimnisvoller Bauchredner aus der Mitte der Leinwand den hörbaren Part ihrer stummen Reden übernimmt.‹[4]

Die Möglichkeiten der Tonaufnahme ziehen den »Schatten« vom Gegenstand ab und lassen ihn in seinem eigenen Recht existieren. Das ist die Geburtsstunde der *musique concrète*. Die allgemeine Verfügbarkeit von Tonband lädt seit den 50er Jahren zum Herumspielen ein. Und einmal losgelassen, hängt der Ton sich an alle möglichen Dinge – die unmöglichen eingeschlossen. Spontan, unwiderstehlich und ohne logische Grundlage gehen Bild und Ton im Geiste eine Beziehung ein im Zeichen des Synchrontons: vorausgesetzt allein, Bild und Ton erfolgen zu exakt demselben Zeitpunkt. Diese Möglichkeit, zu trennen und zu mischen, ist essentiell für den Tonfilm.

Die machtvollste Position darin hat die Stimme des Abwesenden inne, des noch nicht sichtbar gewordenen Körpers, des acousmêtre. In seiner Ortlosigkeit ist es zum einen mit einer besonderen Allmacht ausgestattet[5] und kann zum anderen als exemplarisch gelten für die ›Stimme, die zum Körper will‹ – eine Bewegung, in deren Zeichen die gesamte Geschichte des Kinos gelesen werden kann: »the history of film […] as an endless movement of integrating the most disparate elements: sound and image, the sensory and the verbal.«[6]

Jedoch – in Anbetracht der Videoarbeiten von Matthias Meyer ausgerechnet auf die Stimme zu sprechen zu kommen, ist das nicht eine geistige Entgleisung? Wenn bei einem Artefakt von hohem Bekanntheitsgrad systematisch etwas entfernt worden ist, und zwar auf der Ebene des Bildes – dann ausgerechnet nach dem zu fragen, was derweil die Ebene des Tons anbietet, oder besser gesagt: vorenthält – nämlich z. B. den Ton selbst?

Matthias Meyer arbeitet mit dem Material oder ausgewählten Sequenzen aus längst kanonisch gewordenen cineastischen Kinoproduktionen oder Kunstfilmen: Michelangelo Antonionis *Blowup*, Méliès' *Voyage dans la lune*, Chris Markers *La jetée*, Michael Snows *Wavelength*, Jean-Luc Godards *Le mépris*, der *Meuterei auf der Bounty* und *Moby Dick*. Ein wohl bekanntes Bild, sei es bewegt oder nicht, erzeugt als Erinnerung ein deutliches inneres Bild, vielleicht mit unscharfem Rand, oder mit Ungereimtheiten im Detail. Möglicherweise verstellt das, was deutlich hervortritt, anderes, das auf diese Weise nicht gesehen wird. Meyers Videos trennen, was trennbar ist, und arbeiten mit Weglassungen, unter deren Vorzeichen sie jeweils eine Art Zeitreiseeffekte hervorbringen, aber die Stimme, sie kommt dabei nicht vor.

All die Finessen des Synchrontons, das Akusmatische im Chion'schen Sinne etc., spielen für Matthias Meyers Videos eine nur untergeordnete Rolle. Vielmehr ist es die dem zugrundeliegende Trennbarkeit von Bild und Ton an sich, bei der sie ansetzen. Sie arbeiten allenfalls mit Atmo, oder gar keinem Ton, weder Musik noch der menschlichen Stimme.

Die Fragestellung nach dem Ton (der Stimme, dem Menschen) in diesen Videoarbeiten findet unter dem Vorzeichen einer doppelten Verneinung statt: Die Stimme befindet sich im Kino in unmittelbarer Nähe zu Phänomenen wie Seele, Schatten, Doppelgänger als immateriellen Repräsentanten des Körpers, denen man es zutraut, dessen Tod zu überleben. Wo kein Ton, da keine Stimme, wo kein Körper, da keine immaterielle Repräsentanz.

Eine Menge Phantasie muss man schon aufbringen, um den abwesenden Körper, der seine ebenfalls nicht anwesende Stimme erst noch finden soll, zu imaginieren. Ein Phantomtanz in einem leergeräumten Raum.

Spricht man über Sound wie Chion und Murch, dann gelangt man ebenfalls recht bald in ein Vokabular von Abwesenheiten, negativem Raum, Soundvakuum und Lücke, die eine Bereicherung der Bedeutung und Anreicherung der Atmosphäre bedeuten. Murch sieht eine Gefahr des zeitgenössischen Kinos darin gegeben, dass es mit seinen mimetisch-repräsentativen Möglichkeiten seine Gegenstände erdrückt. Denn im Gegensatz zu anderen Künsten, die eine sinnliche

Unvollständigkeit auszeichnet, kommt der Film als ein Medium der Fülle daher.

Vor diesem Hintergrund verbindet die Geschichte von Bild und Ton im Kino zwei gegenläufige Bewegungen. Da gibt es zum einen die Träume von Vereinigung und Zusammenführung, die sich erfüllen wollen. Interessanter ist es aber, jeweils das zu beobachten, was sich ihrer Erfüllung entgegenstellt. »There is no place for completeness« – dies zeichnet für Walter Murch die Theoriebildung Michel Chions aus.[7]

2. Die Leute

»No, this is not drama, this is just change.«
(James Tenney, 1978)

Wie herzlos, sage ich, Junge, dass du einfach die Leute rausnimmst. Und damit meine ich nicht Seele, dass jetzt keine Seele mehr wäre in der Kunst, Seele das geht mir etwas zu weit, das ist mir zu simpel und zu hochtrabend, aber die Verhältnisse zwischen den Leuten, die Verhältnisse, in denen all das stattfindet, wovon der Film erzählt. Und jetzt komm mir nicht damit, du interessierst dich nicht für die Erzählung, was ein Film dir erzählt, macht dich fertig, dich darauf konzentrieren zu sollen, das macht dich nervenkrank, deshalb liest du auch, wenn es sich irgendwie vermeiden lässt, kein Buch, aber es ist doch wohl so, dass auch jenseits der Geschichte, die der Film in irgendeiner Weise ja doch zumeist rüberbringt, wie man es von ihm erwartet für das an der Kinokasse entrichtete Eintrittsgeld, auch ohne diese also erzählen die Dinge und Bilder und Leute und die Bilder der Leute von sich selbst und den Dingen, mit denen sie sich umgeben, allerhand von ihren Verhältnissen, was hingegen gar nicht mehr erscheint oder nur noch sehr schwer zu entziffern ist, wenn du von allem, was in dem Film war, am Ende nur ausgerechnet den Garten der Natur noch stehen lässt, in dem die ganze Sache sich abspielt, und eine Ladung unspezifischen, nichtmenschlichen Ton.

Oder?

Mitgetilgt sind ja auch weitestgehend erzählerische Strategien und Konnotationen.

Dem Ding eine Subjektivität verpassen und sehen, ob es sie bei sich behält.

Um die Lücken zu füllen, die auftauchen, während die Bestandteile eines Dispositivs sich scheinbar selbsttätig realisieren.

Ein geschwärztes Gemälde ist auch nicht einfach ein schwarzes Bild (und schon gar nicht kein Bild), ohne nicht zugleich auch kein Malewitsch zu sein.

Jemand, der nicht spricht, ist nicht jemand ohne Stimme, und wieder etwas anderes ist ein Stummfilm, wieder anders einer ohne Ton.

If in doubt – leave it out.

Was zurückbleibt, ist gelegentlich eine desillusionierende Ödheit; aber auch die Desillusionierung ist nicht perfekt.

Der gesamte Text von »À rebours«, Buchstabe für Buchstabe auf die Leinwand projiziert, ist auch nicht einfach nur eine nahezu unleserlich gemachte

Variante eines ohnehin schon über Strecken schwer leserlichen Textes, aufgeblasen auf die mehr als vierfache Länge von Andy Warhols *Empire.*

[Internet Movie Database]: Warning: This synopsis is too short.

Sondern an diesem Nullpunkt der Leserlichkeit

Als KÖNNTE MAN die Elemente des Films addieren und subtrahieren, natürlich kann man das, technisch gesehen geht das, aber was ergibt es für einen Sinn?

Bedeutung ist auch nicht so einfach zu eliminieren.

Unansehbare Werke, das Ungeschehenmachen von Bücherverbrennungen

Als Abwehrmechanismus verstanden, bewirken beim Ungeschehenmachen eine Art magischer Handlungen, dass eine vorhergegangene Handlung nicht stattgefunden hat; gegenteiliges Handeln hebt die ursprüngliche Handlung auf. So läuft das hier nicht.

Beim Magischen treten Illusion und Desillusion beide mit Perfektionsanspruch auf, um ihr Gelingen sicherzustellen.

Matthias Meyer interessiert das nicht. Ein dezidierter Nichtleser, erscheint der Künstler als Wiesel, als Hase und Igel, die selbstverständlich beide unsichtbar bleiben.

So stellen sich manche Befunde im Konditional ein: was wäre, wenn? Was wäre das, wenn es das gäbe?

Desillusion – das interessiert ihn nicht. Oder auch der berühmte Blick hinter die Kulissen, zum Beispiel des Louvre, verbleibt in den Kulissen selbst und beleiht deren Aura.

Etwas tritt in die Lücke. Ein Verschwinden, Versickern und ein deutliches Bild davon.

Die Fragen, die sich aufwerfen, betreffen vielmehr das Feld der Wahrnehmung als das der Wahrheit. Man müsste sich verbiegen, um das wahrzunehmen; mit den Wahrnehmungsapparaten yogische Verbiegungspositionen einnehmen.

Ist man einmal so weit, sich selbst als Subjekt als zusammengesetzt zu betrachten, oder als zerstreut, aber zusammensetzbar, und ebenso den Sound im Kino als etwas vom Körper Getrenntes, das mit diesem in keineswegs notwendigen festen Beziehungen steht und also davon abgelöst werden kann und, zumindest mit Hilfe der dazu notwendigen und zur Verfügung stehenden Apparate, auch wieder zusammengesetzt, und zwar immer anders zusammengesetzt, und dass darin auch eine Freiheit gesehen werden kann und nicht nur eine Bedrohung, oder dass jede Freiheit, die man begreift, eine Bedrohung und eine Verunsicherung darstellt, aber dass es auch möglich sein kann, die Verunsicherung zu wünschen und sie nicht nur zu fliehen wie der Teufel angeblich das Weihwasser, dann kann man in diesen neu entstandenen Spielräumen der Zusammensetzbarkeit und Rekombinierbarkeit auch anfangen zu spielen. Matthias Meyer will nicht spielen. Er öffnet diese Räume und löst das Trennbare voneinander ab, aber er beginnt nicht zu spielen. Ihm ist es lieber, die Räume bleiben leer. Ihm ist es lieber, wenn keine Menschen darin sind, und wenn Geister, selbst dann auch nur die Geister der Geister, die Geister in ihrer Abwesenheit. Abgesehen von den Apparaten, die bestimmte Dinge (Bild, Ton, Subjektivität) ermöglichen, und zwar für gewöhnlich unter der Voraussetzung ihrer eigenen Unwahrnehmbarkeit, hat es Matthias Meyer die Atmosphäre angetan. Jene Apparate können durch die Trennung des Trennbaren selbst zur Darstellung kommen. Doch was ist mit der Atmosphäre? Der Begriff lässt nicht von uns ab. Wenn zwei oder mehr Menschen sich über die Atmosphäre unterhalten, die irgendwo geherrscht habe, worüber reden sie dann? Ein kategorisch unscharfer Begriff, zu dessen Klärung bislang wenig Versuche unternommen wurden; technisches Konzept der Tongestaltung, gasförmige Hülle eines Himmelkörpers.

Die Metapher wäre ein mögliches Spiel, dessen Begriff Walter Murch auch auf die Ebene des Tons anwendet, und deren Hervorbringung einen Wahrnehmungsfreiraum schafft, der dem

»Alles-da« des Films entgegensteht und verhindert, dass er mit Überfülle seinen Gegenstand erschlägt. Stattdessen wird ein Mehrwert in der Rezeption ermöglicht. Mit Aristoteles sagt Murch von der Metapher, dass sie »ein Ding bei dem benennt, was nicht sein Name ist«, ein schöner Phantomtanz auch das.

3. Niemand
»Every place has its own silence.«
(Michel Chion, 1991)

(*Empty Moon for an Empty Room*) Niemand landet auf dem Mond. Das ergibt ein in sich flackerndes knatterndes Bild. Am Horizont geht nicht die Erde auf und taucht das Geschehen in ein unwirkliches Licht. Diese ganz und unteilbar wirkende Kraterlandschaft muss doch zur einen Hälfte hinter der anderen versenkbar sein.

Da ist ein Ort, den noch nie ein Mensch gesehen hat, der Regisseur Georges Méliès nicht und niemand sonst, nicht nur noch nie zuvor, sondern auch jetzt nicht, 1902; es ist ein Werk der Magie, dieses Bild. Das ungesehene Bild, das Bild von etwas Ungesehenem. Das sind Zeitreisen, in andere Zeitschichten des Films. Reisen in die Zeit des Kinos, die Chronik der Kinogeschichte. Was ist denn eine Location? Ein Ort für Ereignisse.

(*Ohne Titel*) Er geht nicht über die Treppe den Hang hinauf Richtung Tatort, erst wie ein Schatten, dann auftauchend aus dem Grün in den diesigen Himmel; ob es Regen gegeben hat oder noch geben wird, ist nicht zu sagen. Und die Bäume rauschen. Kurz bevor er oben ankommt, beschleunigt er nicht seinen Schritt, nimmt auch nicht zwei Stufen auf einmal und biegt zur linken Seite ab, wo ein nicht enden wollender Lattenzaun den weiten Rasen des Maryon Park umfasst.

Er senkt nun nicht, um die Kamera zu richten, die er zwischen seinen Händen dreht, den Blick, und unter dem Wogen des dichten Blattwerks an den Ästen läuft er nicht von links in die Rasenfläche hinein. Er verfällt nicht in den Laufschritt und wendet sich um, ob jemand kommt, und in seinem Gesicht ist nichts von grimmiger Zielstrebigkeit zu lesen. Kein suchender Blick, kein Abtasten der Umgebung, kein Niederhocken bei dem Busch inmitten der Fläche, im sorgfältig geschnittenen Gras. Niemand hat sich vergebens an diesen Ort begeben, die Kamera resigniert auf der Erde abgestützt, und von zwei vereinzelten Zweigen an Haar und Schulter geklopft, vielleicht auch nur sachte von deren Hauch gestreift, den Blick gegen den Himmel gewandt und die rauschenden Kronen der Bäume.

Dabei hat er geglaubt, in den Bildern Evidenz für etwas gefunden zu haben. Ein System von Evidenzen. Er hat das Auge, er beherrscht die Techniken des Hinsehens, es ist seine Profession. Hinter dem Zaun, ein Gesicht. Ein Gesicht ist etwas, das sich aus weißen Bildpunkten zusammensetzt und auch wieder in solche zerfällt. Die Frau hat etwas in ihrem Blick, das ihm Hinweise zu geben scheint. Zwischen den Schusslinien.

Der kaum wahrnehmbare Loop unterstützt eine mikrorhythmische Dynamik des Naturgeschehens im Londoner Maryon Park. Unter »Mikrorhythmen« fasst Michel Chion schnelle Bewegungen auf der Bildoberfläche, die durch Schnee, Rauch, Regen, sich kräuselnde Wasser- oder Sandoberflächen erzeugt werden, oder auch durch die Körnung des Bildes.[8] Diese Elemente schaffen schnelle, flüssige Rhythmuswerte, die eine vibrierende Zeitlichkeit im Bild selbst erzeugen: »It is as if this technique affirms a kind of time proper to sound cinema as a recording of the microstructure of the present.«

Ohne Titel kehrt an den Zeitpunkt zurück, an dem der Tonfilm aus dem Kino eine Zeit-Kunst gemacht hat, und kehrt sein chronographisches Wesen hervor. Denn der Synchronton beeinflusst die Zeitwahrnehmung im Bild. Für den Tonfilm wurde es notwendig, die Projektionsgeschwindigkeit zu stabilisieren. Film ist »written in time«.[9]

Im Tonfilm bewirkt der Sound die Unumkehrbarkeit der Bildfolge und der Zeit, und zwar, wenn etwa Wasser tropft, mit jedem einzelnen Tropfen (ein jeder eine Geschichte für sich).

Schon Musik stiftet eine Dimension von Echtzeit und Linearität; nehmen wir ein Piano: jede Note beginnt zu sterben, sobald sie geboren ist, das sind lauter Indices gerichteter Echtzeit; die gesprochene Stimme aber nimmt endgültig der Zeit die Elastizität, und die Alltagszeit kehrt in den Tonfilm ein.

In *Ohne Titel* dagegen ist die Zeit noch nicht oder nicht mehr vektorisiert.

Zunichte gemacht wird, was Ereignis ist. Statt die Zeit in gerichtete Flugbahnen zu führen, wirkt das Naturgeschehen im Maryon Park eher wie nach Chion die »anemphatische Musik«, die unbeeindruckt vom Geschehen einfach weiterläuft und der mechanischen Natur des Films und seines Abspulens entspricht, das er selbst emphatisch vergessen machen will.[10]

Der Sound stiftet im Erzählkino dem Bild Einheitlichkeit, indem er visuelle Lücken zu überbrücken hilft, und gibt eine atmosphärische Hülle vor, »a framework that seems to contain the image, a ›heard space‹ in which the ›seen‹ bathes.«[11] Bleiben Lücken zurück, die der Sound nicht überbrücken kann, so steht die Hülle als solche dahin. Ein Jump Cut z. B. kann zwei Räume auf paradoxe Weise verbinden, durch die subjektive Figur; fällt diese wie in *Ohne Titel* weg, so fallen auch die Räume auseinander und auf sich selbst zurück. Was geschieht da? Vielleicht in einer Art Umkehrung des Phantasmas vom absoluten Gegenschuss, nämlich der Idee, der Filmcharakter würde nun uns sehen können, wie bisher wir ihn, dass nun unser eigener Platz als Betrachtende leer wird? Eine so weitgehende Räumung …

Das Vogelgezwitscher, das zu hören ist, ist synonym für das, was man gerne hören würde, da man gerade hinhört; aber dort ist nichts; niemand horcht auf auf der Suche nach Hinweisen, nichts als das Zwitschern der Vögel und der ewige Wind, den nichts und niemand in einem Raum mit präzisen Abmessungen festzusetzen in der Lage ist.

(*Beaufort*) Niemand hängt in den Seilen. Niemand wird geschlagen. Die Schläge würden von einem Geräusch begleitet werden, das unseren Glauben an sie unterstützt. Niemand unter Deck im Bauch des Schiffes begehrt auf. Niemand befährt die sieben Meere. Keine 5 000 Eingeborenen von sechs Südseeinseln kommen zum Einsatz in einem außergewöhnlichen Cast. Innenräume, Außenräume, alle auf derselben Distanz. Kein Teleporter vermittelt zwischen diesen Bühnen. (Das wäre dann der Mensch).

Jemand muss ja da sein. (Jemand mit einer Filmkamera). (Versuchen wir, die Lücke zu schließen). Ein Schiff ist eine Insel. Eine Welt der toten Dinge, jenseits ihres Gebrauchs. Für sich genommen sinnlos, und ohne Ton. Die über den Schiffskarten schaukelnde Lampe wäre üblicher-

weise ein stummer Moment in einem Tonfilm.
Eine solche »Stille« muss natürlich tontechnisch
eigens hergestellt werden; die Stille ein Resonanz-
moment, eingebettet in einen kontinuierlichen
Hintergrundton (von Meer, Möwen, Fischen).
Stummfilm, in den die Zeit noch nicht Einzug
gehalten hat. Oder als wäre nichts geschehen:
nach Auszug der Zeit. Jemand sieht das. Keine
Andeutung über Art, Ursache und Zeitpunkt
des Abhandenkommens.

Hier haben keine Kämpfe stattgefunden,
oder schon vor sehr langer Zeit. Es sind Bilder
einer aufmerksamen Begehung, die auf einen
fragwürdigen Kontext verweisen (vielleicht nach
Jahrzehnten, verloren geglaubt, in einer rostigen
Filmdose in einem Kinokeller irgendwo in einem
südamerikanischen Land wiederaufgetaucht),
anders gesagt, die Frage aufwerfen nach Kontext
überhaupt.

(*Ghost*) Er kommt nicht durch die, obwohl
ewig der Sonneneinstrahlung ausgesetzt, immer
noch grünen Büsche aus den Felsen hinabgelaufen,
im Anzug, die linke Hand in der Hosentasche
vergraben wie ein Typ in einem Film. Der es nicht
nötig hat, die Hände frei zu haben, wenn er aus

schwindelerregender Höhe irgendwo nach unten herabsteigt.

Durch die in die jahrtausendealte Natur eingelassene Architektur eines mit Mauern befestigten Serpentinenweges hat er nun nicht den Weg in Gegenrichtung eingeschlagen. Er nicht, und auch kein anderer, der sich nun in seiner Begleitung befände, hemdsärmlig und ebenfalls in sommerheller Kleidung, und nun durch die vom Weg vollzogene Wendung schlagartig in ein Reich der Schatten eingetreten wäre, Blätterdach und Kühle und eine Abdunkelung des Lichts, durch die erst verstehbar geworden wäre die Unbarmherzigkeit der Sonne zuvor.

Wie so manches durch die Helle des Tages, durch die Ungeschütztheit des Auges sichtbar geworden ist.

»In the cinema, to look is to explore, at once spatially and temporally, in a ›given-to-see‹ (field of vision) that has limits contained by the screen. But […] the aural field is much less limited or confined, its contours uncertain and changing.«[12]

Eben erst würde er begriffen haben, dass er vorher seine Augen gern geschützt haben würde, dass er vorher eine Brille hätte getragen haben wollen, wenn er eine dabei gehabt hätte, hätte er denn daran gedacht.

Dort unten wie ein Gürteltier aus Stein, das Haus, hoch über dem Wasser, von drei Seiten uneinnehmbar, erreichbar über die vierte.

Das Dach ist kein Dach ist eine Treppe und Dach zugleich, sein Kopf und seine Schultern kein Kopf und keine Schultern im Treppablaufen, Treppe und Dach sind unscharf getrennt, Treppenfunktion und Dachfunktion kippen an dieser Stelle, aus dieser Warte ineinander über.

Das sagt niemand: Schöne gelbe Farbe. Und niemand: Danke.

Niemand geht durchs Bild. Wobei Wellen auf Felsen schlagen und verwaschenes Tiergeräusch an die Ohren dringt, Möwen. Niemand geht über das Dach. Aber ich meine, Schritte zu hören. Jemand würde übers Dach gehen, wäre diesen Hang hinabgekommen, könnte in diesem Fenster sitzen. In einer anderen Zeit. Das jetzt lautere Aufbrausen der See. Mit seinem Geräusch sind auch die außerhalb der Bilder liegenden Grenzen dieses Raumes gegeben, alles, was sich darin befindet, ist definiert als diesseits, hier. In die Koordinaten der durch die Bauten gegebenen

Räume sind so unverrückbar die Orte einge-
spannt, welche die Figuren darin einnehmen müssen. Die Atmo schafft einen Raum von keiner
benennbaren Tiefe, irgendwie synthetisch, kunst-
stofflich. Weniger, als den Raum zu definieren,
ist sie vielmehr selbst dieser Raum.

(*The Black Museum*) Nun werden Bilder ge-
schwärzt, entfernt und davongetragen. Hier sind
Menschen, aber kein Ton. Schweigefilm? Stummfilm? Sie reden nicht. Da der Film selbst hoch-
gradig Bild ist, muss es sich wohl um zwei Ord-
nungen von Bildern handeln und es kommt eine
gehobene Stimmung auf. Die RestauratorInnen
bessern das Schwarz aus. DoppelgängerInnen des
Künstlers, haben sie etwas Naseweises, wie sie
an die Finessen des Schwarz herangehen. Im Kino
ist Bild gleich Frame, der im Fall eine Spielfilms
hunderte Einstellungen und zehntausende Einzel-
bilder enthält. Was also »Bild« ist im Kino, bezeichnet nicht den Inhalt, sondern den Behälter,
und kann als solcher schwarz und leer sein. Gerade wenn es als Schwarzbild leer bleibt, ist es keine
Abwesenheit und kein Nichts, sondern recht-
eckig, gefüllt und sichtbar zum Betrachten präsent.
So bestätigt der Frame sich selbst als vorgängiger

Container, der auch bleiben wird, nachdem die Bilder gegangen sein werden, eine Dimension des schwarzen Bildes, die der Nachspann beim Spielfilm gewissermaßen aufrechterhält.[13] Wenn an einer Stelle in *The Black Museum* die MuseumsarbeiterInnen ein riesiges Schwarz wie einen Vorhang oder Teppich über die Bildfläche ziehen bis über die äußersten Ränder des Frames hinaus, comicfigurenhafte Garanten dafür, das der Laden läuft, kippen Bild und Rahmen ineinander, und es darf gelacht werden.

(*No Empire*) Empire – die Wortvorstellung allein – erhält die Erhabenheit noch des von Andy Warhols Ansicht des Empire State Building geleerten Bildes aufrecht und bezeichnet des Weiteren auch dieses Reich der Sinne dort auf der Leinwand sowie die Grenzen jenes Reiches. Welche Grenzen könnten das sein?

Der nächtliche Himmel, das flackernde Grau, der schwarze Himmel. Das, was die Erde umgibt als Hülle – Atmosphäre. Hier, wo Gegenstand des Films das ungegenständliche Element schlechthin ist, fallen auf völlig überraschende Weise Materialität des Films und Figürlichkeit im Begriff der Atmosphäre in eins.

An- und Abwesenheit, das ist in diesem Reich, wie in dem der Geister, kein Widerspruch mehr. Und apropos Geister: Einige von ihnen pflegen ein verschwommenes Aussehen, andere lassen sich am besten im Modus der Unschärfe fangen.

4. Sieh dir diese Bilder einmal scharf an!

Schon wieder betrachte ich Nebel, die am Fenster vorübertreiben, Rauch oder Schneeverwehungen, Dinge, über deren Ursprung ich mir nicht im Klaren bin und deren Namen ich nicht kenne; schon wieder führen mich meine so genannten Studien zum Schatten, der vom Körper abgetrennt ist, und dem Verhältnis zwischen Bild und Ton. Was wäre, wenn es Menschen gäbe?

Etwas hält mich davon ab, ich kann es nicht benennen.

In Matthias Meyers Arbeit *A Museum of Its Memory* sind übereinander belichtet zu sehen sämtliche Bilder von Chris Markers fast durchgängig in fotografischen Einzelbildern erzähltem

Experimentalfilm *La jetée*, somit alle Bilder des Films auf ein einziges zurückführend. Wirklich zu sehen ist das nicht. Zu sehen ist ein Grau, das nichts mehr abbildet, ein Unschärfebildraum unklarer Herkunft.

Betrachtet man wiederum *Folded Fog*, eine 4 mal 3 Meter große computergenerierte Grisaille, deren zweites Hauptmerkmal ihre Zusammenfaltbarkeit ist, lassen sich Anklänge an eine ästhetische Tradition der Unschärfe nicht übersehen, die bis vor die Wende zum 20. Jahrhundert zurückreicht. Aus der Malerei entlehnte Landschaftserfahrungen, auf das Genre der Fotografie übertragen, gingen darin einher mit einer hohen poetischen wie kunsttheoretischen Wertschätzung von Phänomenen wie Nebel, Mondlicht und Dämmerung. Mit dem Nebel und seiner »natürlichen Unschärfe«, so Wolfgang Ullrich, löste sich deren Geltungsbereich vom abgebildeten Objekt und wurde unabhängig vom Sujet.[14] Im Einklang mit zeitgenössischen Stimmungsbedürfnissen, die mit einer Ablehnung der Stofflichkeit der Dinge korrespondieren, vernichtet die Weichzeichnerfotografie durch Lichtentzug oder aber Überstrahlung die Plastizität der Gegenstände bis hin zur Dreidimensionalität des Raumes selbst und verwandelt diesen in einen reinen Stimmungsraum. Um diese Wirkung zu erzielen, bedarf es allerdings innerhalb des verschwindenden Raumes immer noch scharfer Gegenstände, Gegenstandsreste oder Kontraste, die ihrem Verschwinden vorausgehen. Zwar bilden Matthias Meyers Unschärfebilder, frei von derartigen Residuen, insofern solche Stimmungsräume gerade nicht, und es ist gerade ihre eigene, ansonsten verborgene Stofflichkeit, auf die sie zurückführen; dennoch wäre es absurd, die Sujets von *Folded Fog*, *No Empire* und *A Museum of Its Memory* von jener Ästhetik des weichgezeichneten Bildes vollends abzuschneiden, die dem Blick in die Ferne entspricht, »der alles und nichts umschließt«, mit dem Fernziel, »sich in einem Bild wiederzufinden«.[15] Vielmehr wird im Gegenzug die romantisch-antimoderne Haltung, die in jener Tradition Gestalt annimmt, durch eine Reise in die Zeit des stummen Films auf die Füße gestellt, wenn etwa in *Empty Moon for an Empty Room* der von menschlichen Besuchern leer geräumte Mond des Georges Méliès daran erinnert, dass es Kinozeiten gab, in denen es möglich wurde, Bilder

tatsächlich zu betreten, dieser uralte Wunsch-
traum der Menschen. Die Versprechen der Möglichkeiten von Film, revisited.

Die Unschärfen symbolistischer Malerei, mit
der verborgene, wahrere Welten angerufen werden;[16] die besonderen Kräfte des Mediums, die
das fotografische Bild in seiner Anfangszeit noch
als ein Werk besonderer Magie erscheinen ließen
und aus diesem Grund auch als privilegiertes
Medium für den Umgang mit Geistern – die
Dimension des Okkulten hallt sicherlich, ebenso
wie der Gedanke an die Stimme der Toten, der
insbesondere mit der Frühzeit von Telefon und
Grammophon verbunden ist, auch in den Un-
schärfephänomenen bei Matthias Meyer nach.
Nur spielt das Problem der Wahrnehmung in
seinen Arbeiten eine sehr viel größere Rolle als
das der Wahrheit.

Und vor dem *Folded Fog* fehlt die Caspar
David Friedrich'sche Rückenfigur, als Mittler in
den Bildraum: Da ist er wieder, nicht.

Man kann in diese Bilder nur von ihrer Geschichte und Tradition her einsteigen, so dass
man sieht, was man sieht, und was nicht. So
kommt es, dass selbst Arbeiten wie *No Empire*,

wo aus Andy Warhols ohnehin schon maximal reduziertem *Empire* das Empire State Building auch noch durchgängig entfernt wurde, ebenso wie *A Museum of Its Memory*, auf den reinen Rohstoff ihrer Materialität zurückgeführt, noch Spuren einer Gegenständlichkeit tragen.

Die traditionelle unscharfe Fotografie, ob sie nun innere Bilder nachschaffen wollte[17] oder dem allsehenden Auge eine entgrenzte Anschauung, misst ihre Gegenstände am Maßstab ästhetischer Autonomie. Dagegen rufen die Unschärfe- und Leerräume bei Matthias Meyer, welche die gegenständliche, subjekthafte, sprechende Welt zugleich sowohl zu absorbieren wie freizusetzen scheinen, Kontexte geradezu notwendig herbei, sich in diese einzubinden.

5. Nachtrag: Ein denkbar deutliches Bild

Zu ergänzen wäre noch, unter Wiederaufnahme einzelner Motive, die zu einem erratischen »Werk«-Zusammenhang zusammentreten, eine ganze Liste von Sujets, die aufzutauchen und zu verschwinden vermögen und dabei im Vorüber- oder Untergehen ein denkbar deutliches Bild abgeben. *The Rising Snow / The Falling Stars* ist ein sprechender Titel dieser Doppelbewegung. In deren Sinn nun auch die Stimme zur Ansicht kommt: Unter dem Titel einer Fragestellung (»How can you smile when you're deep in thought?«), die Morton Feldman und John Cage 1966 in einer Radiosendung diskutierten, verschwindet die Stimme im selben Moment ihrer Vergegenwärtigung. Was Feldman und Cage dort über den Stellenwert der Idee in der künstlerischen Arbeit, über das Konzept Künstler und das Konzept Idee erörtern, überführt Matthias Meyer als Klang der Sprechmelodien beider Künstlerstimmen in rein musikalischen Ton, gespielt von einem Vibraphon, und legt es des Weiteren in schriftlicher Form als Partitur nieder. In vielfältiger Umkehr der Verhältnisse von Notierung und Ausführung, Konzeption und Performance, zieht sich diskret die Stimme zurück in Musik.

Das selbstspielende Klavier *Index* wiederum, in einer Installation gemeinsam dargeboten mit dem kinoleinwandgroßen Wandbild *Folded Fog*, spielt die Mondscheinsonate von Beethoven gerade *nicht*. Vielmehr gibt es sehr langsam und nach einem bestimmten arithmetischen Schlüssel das gesamte Toninventar des Musikstückes wieder. Bild und Ton keines eigentlichen Films, bringen Nebel und Leinwand einerseits, das Klavier im emphatischen, um nicht zu sagen, im Loriot'schen Sinne andererseits, vignettenartig die hergebrachte Aura im Moment ihre Verlustiggehens zur Anschauung.

In einer Parkecke wiederum ein kleiner Strudel aus schwarzer Tinte: ein schwarzes Loch, das sich permanent selbst verschluckt und zugleich wieder hervorbringt. Reminiszenz seinerseits an die Schallplattenaufnahme mit dem Titel *The Whirl*: Dort befindet sich der spiralförmige Verlauf der Tonrille auf dem schwarzen Vinyl in perfekter Korrespondenz mit einer Aufzählung all jener Gegenstände, die sich in Edgar Allan Poes »Maelstrom«-Erzählung, im Untergang begriffen, in einer wie ewig andauernden, rasenden Schwebe an der Innenseite des Wirbelstroms halten.

1   Vgl. Michel Chion, *Audio-Vision: Sound on Screen*, hg. u. übers. v. Claudia Gorbman, Vorwort von Walter Murch. New York 1994. [frz. *L'audio-vision* 1991]

2   Michel Chion, *The Voice in Cinema*, hg. u. übers. v. Claudia Gorbman. New York 1999. [frz. *La voix au cinéma* 1982]

3   Vgl. Walter Murch, Vorwort zu *Audio-Vision: Sound on Screen*, a. a. O., S. viii.

4   Vgl. Chion, *The Voice in Cinema*, S. 131, Übers. d. A.

5   Chion, *The Voice in Cinema*, S. 24: »The one you don't see is in the best position to see you.« Aufgrund der panoptischen Allmacht des »Acousmêtre« begleitet dieses häufig eine paranoide, auch obsessive Phantasie. Michel Chion spricht von der ›alles sehenden Stimme‹.

6   Chion, *Audio-Vision: Sound on Screen*, S. 183

7   Murch, Vorwort zu *Audio-Vision: Sound on Screen*, S. xxiv

8   Chion, *Audio-Vision: Sound on Screen*, S. 16

9   Chion, *Audio-Vision: Sound on Screen*, S. 17

10 Chion, *Audio-Vision: Sound on Screen*, S. 9

11 Chion, *Audio-Vision: Sound on Screen*, S. 47

12 Chion, *Audio-Vision: Sound on Screen*, S. 33

13 Vgl. Chion, *Audio-Vision: Sound on Screen*, 66f.

14 Vgl. zum Folgenden Wolfgang Ullrich, *Die Geschichte der Unschärfe*. Berlin 2002, 2009. Hier S. 19

15 Vgl. Ullrich, *Die Geschichte der Unschärfe*, S. 42

16 Vgl. Ullrich, *Die Geschichte der Unschärfe*, S. 48f.

17 Vgl. Ullrich, *Die Geschichte der Unschärfe*, S. 98

Ohne Titel
1999/2007
2-Kanal-Videoprojektion
13:19 Min.

Ohne Titel basiert auf den subjektiven
Kameraeinstellungen der zentralen Szenen
aus Michelangelo Antonionis Film *Blowup*
(1966), in denen der Fotograf ein Liebespaar
im Londoner Maryon Park fotografiert und
dabei unbewusst Zeuge eines Mordes wird.

    Alle Personen der Handlung sind
herausretuschiert. Die Doppelprojektion
zeigt nur noch den im Wind rauschenden
Park. Durch die digitale Ausblendung und
die Konstruktion einer Leerstelle erlangt
die im Fokus des Originalfilms stehende
Problematik filmischer Bildrealität eine ver-
schärfte Präsenz.

Saved from Fire (1–3)
2007/2008
Bücher, Holz
Größe variabel

François Truffauts Verfilmung aus dem
Jahr 1966 von Ray Bradburys Roman
Fahrenheit 451 bildet die Vorlage für die
Auswahl der Bücher in den drei Regal-
objekten *Saved from Fire*. Die im Film
verbrannten Bücher, sind hier unversehrt
versammelt und scheinen durch Raum
und Zeit gerettet.

À rebours
2008
1-Kanal-Videoprojektion
34:43:50 Std.

Mit Joris-Karl Huysmans' *Gegen den Strich* (1884)
hat Matthias Meyer erstmals einen reinen Textfilm
konzipiert, bei dem die einzelnen Buchstaben des
Romans in der Mitte des Bildes nacheinander ablau-
fen. Das Buch wird in der französischen Originalfas-
sung quasi buchstabiert, sodass es trotzdem lesbar
bleibt. Die Dauer der Projektion übersteigt natürlich
die Aufmerksamkeit des Betrachters; Langsamkeit
spielt bei Huysmans jedoch eine wichtige Rolle: Der
dekadente, aristokratische Protagonist Jean Floressas
Des Esseintes führt am liebsten seine mit Juwelen
besetzte Schildkröte spazieren. Im Gegensatz zum
Roman, der eine wortgewaltige Innenschau in die
künstliche Welt von Des Esseintes ist, der immer
neue sinnliche Reize erfindet, um der Langeweile
der Wirklichkeit zu entfliehen, ist Meyers Film eine
minimalistische Versuchsanordnung, die sämtliche
filmische Mittel zugunsten der Sprache negiert.
Die Reduktion von Atmosphäre auf die Buchstaben
des Alphabets bedeutet aber nicht das Verschwinden des Romans, sondern seine Übertragung in eine
formale Struktur, in welcher der unabschließbare
Prozess der subjektiven Wahrnehmung an die Stelle
eindeutiger Informationsvermittlung tritt. Doch
es geht Matthias Meyer nicht nur darum, die Syntax
des Films in seine Bestandteile zu zerlegen oder in
der exponierten Präsentation einzelner semantischer
Schichten ein größeres Ganzes zu evozieren, das in
der kinematografischen oder literarischen Referenz
selbst nur fragmentarisch formuliert ist. Der Prozess
der Dekomposition bringt seinerseits Werke hervor,
die auf klar benennbaren Strukturen basieren, als
solche jedoch rätselhaft bleiben.

Vanessa Joan Müller
(»Non plus d'histoire(s)…«, Auszug)

A Museum of Its Memory
2009
Fotoprint auf Barytpapier
13 × 18 cm

In *A Museum of Its Memory* erfährt der
Film *La jetée* (1962) von Chris Marker eine
Rückführung auf seinen fotografischen
Ursprung. Die 566 Einzelfotos des Original-
films wurden durch Überlagerung in eine
einzige fotografische Schicht belichtet, wo-
bei die Deckkraft jedes einzelnen Bildes der
Erscheinungsdauer im Film entspricht.

Endless Ocean
2009
Holz, Piezoprint
94 × 17 × 19 cm

Eine gerollte und so in sich geschlossene
Seekarte, bei der alle Navigationslinien,
Grade und Koordinaten ihres Zeichen-
systems wie bei einem Möbiusband inein-
anderlaufen. Es gibt keinen Anfang und
kein Ende.

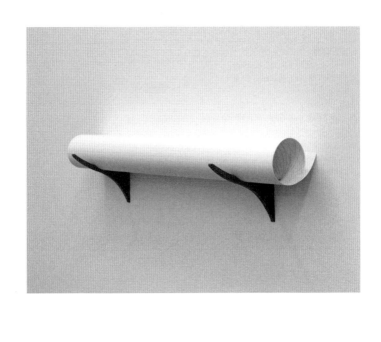

No Empire
2006
1-Kanal-Videoprojektion
60:00 Min., Loop

Andy Warhols Film *Empire* ohne das
Empire State Building. Was bleibt sind
der nächtliche Himmel über New York,
Schmutz, Staub und Kratzer sowie die
Belichtungsfehler auf dem vom Haupt-
motiv befreiten Filmmaterial.

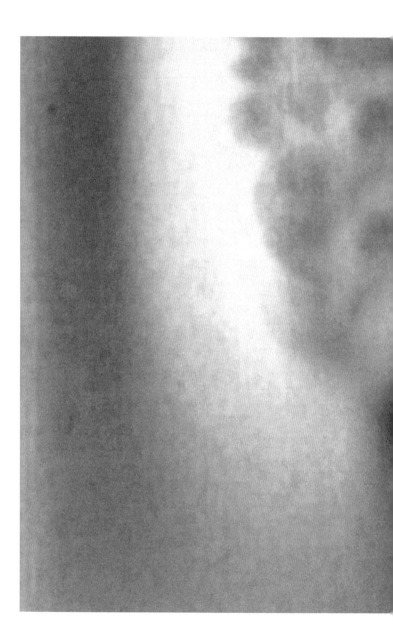

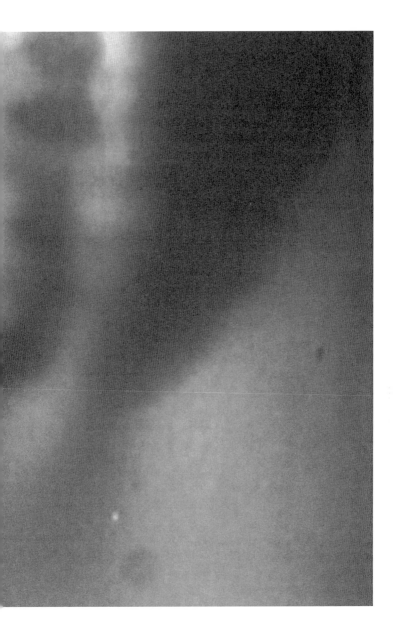

No Call For Brilliant Colour

–

An Incomplete Screenplay

Giles Bailey

*The screen remains dark for a few seconds
until a mechanical click is heard.*

*Extremely close shot of a record player's stylus
poised above a spinning disk. The whir of the belt is
audible. A second click and the needle descends,
settling in the grove of the record. Following characteristic crackles the music begins. It is Giuseppe Di
Stefano singing »Una Furtiva Lagrima«. There is
a sudden atmospheric shift as the opening credits come
up and are set against a series of fleeting images apparently from various times and various locations.
A blank cork surface. Hands appear before the camera and pin a dark image to the pin board, just as
the thumbs leave the corners the shot cuts before the
image is revealed. Tongs turn photographs as they
are bathed in chemicals, the screen flooded with the
scarlet light of the dark room. Close ups of ripples
and light playing across the red liquid. Swift tracking
shot across extensive bookshelves, the titles illegible,
the camera slows and follows bases of the worn
coloured spines. It drifts over a desk, upon which is
a snub-barreled revolver, pans of watercolour paints,
a framed photographic portrait not quite in focus.
A woman carefully folds lengths of black and grey*

*cloth. Close ups of sun-bleached decaying plaster,
a full stop, a paint brush swirled in water, a dried
beech leaf used as bookmark, the nebulae in the crema
of a cup of black coffee. The shapes of a couple as they
walk down a beach, backlit by the sun as sets or rises.
Milk bubbling over the top of a glass as it is blown
into with a straw. The record player again, the stylus
reaching the middle of the track. The music fades.*

*INT. THE WRITER'S APARTMENT.
A EUROPEAN CITY. EVENING*

*A woman's voice is heard.
As she speaks: close shot tracking the length of an
orange plastic Pentel on a wooden desk. Similarly
close shots moving across plain writing paper and
note book pages. Squares, lines, red margins. Other
accoutrements of the writing desk are studied by the
camera. A glass of water, the rings of coffee stains
on a photocopied document, a pair of orange pens
bound with an elastic band the same brand as the
first, paper clips, contorted staples.*

THE WRITER *off*: I've been struggling with this
pen because it feels so comfortable in my hand.

When it reaches the end of whatever it is I've been writing I have to place it back on the desk and face up to what I've become responsible for on the page. While I'm writing I don't like to put it down because I'm frightened that the spell will be broken. I carry it with me when I pause to make a cup of coffee or go to the toilet and I will sit there rolling it between my fingers until it's time to return to work. At moments of particularly high pressure or particularly acute anxiety I carry a spare in the breast pocket of my blouse in order that, should the one with which I'm writing run dry, it can be instantly replaced without having to root around in a draw or go through pockets of a coat discarded on the kitchen table. So I'm both tyrannized by it and reliant on it, as if it were a security blanket. Naturally, coming with that is a deep distrust of my word processor and it sits largely unused like a redundant piece of dutifully inherited furniture. So with this pen, and its arsenal of brothers in my breast pocket or at the stationary shop, comes the certainty that I can write. I did a great deal of research before settling on this particular brand and I made sure that the ink is so indelible that no quantity of beverages spilled across the manuscript will erase it. Nor will the words mysteriously disperse into the ether as they might when the computer crashes or its power cable is tugged accidentally from the wall. But this absurd disclaimer is really just a means of introducing two characters born of this family of pens and committed to the page. One thing that distinguishes them and perhaps makes them worthy of note is their ability to traverse space and time at will irrespective of distance or direction. Whether it is at their will or not remains unclear but it happens nonetheless. We see them here.

EXT. RAILWAY STATION. ANOTHER CITY. NIGHT.
Long shot of a couple, a man and a woman, in dramatic silhouette walking away from the camera arm in arm. They are haloed in the light that pours from streetlights through the arched walkway beneath the track. Steam or fog hangs in wisps. Slow zoom out to show another couple watching them at a distance seated on a bench. They rise and walk away together in conversation. The camera pulls away, following them to reveal they are on a film set. They leave the artificially darkened hanger, stepping

carefully over cables and weaving among crew. They
walk into blinding daylight. Behind them they leave
technicians working as fog billows from machines
and fans disperse it around the space. The camera,
clearly part of the studio rises on a mechanical arm
to give a bird's eye view. The lighting gives some
illusion of black and white film.

The character to the left is myself and the other is,
well, somebody else.

The music swells again and second series of images
begins. Medium tracking shot along a table in a
wood-paneled college conference room about which
Scholars are seated. They appear to animatedly
discuss and gesture toward something not visible to
the left of the frame. Long shot of an office where
many administrators work assiduously. Close shot
of two people discussing something on a desktop
computer screen obscured by their heads. Shot appa-
rently from within a sealed environment of a labora-
tory. Technicians handle something by inserting
their arms through holes in the wall of the environ-
ment into specially attached rubber gloves. The
subject of their attentions is almost entirely out of

the frame. Whatever it is there is the implication
that it is black, sinister and strangely intangible.
Close shot from without the sealed environment of
technician working, arms in the holes to the elbow.
The music fades.

INT. THE METRO. DAY OR NIGHT
THE WRITER and her COMPANION sit
together two or three other travelers are in the
carriage.

THE WRITER *off*: It's clear they are companions but not necessarily lovers.

THE COMPANION: What's that?
He points to a box held on the writer's lap.

THE WRITER: It's a box.
She studies it.
It's wrapped in brown paper and I think it's made of cardboard
Taps it experimentally.

THE COMPANION: Did you have it before we got on?

THE WRITER *distractedly*: Umm.

THE COMPANION: What's in it?

THE WRITER: I don't know.

> *EXT. A CLOUDLESS BLUE SKY. DAY.*
> *The calls of birds.*
>
> *EXT. A PARK. DAY.*
> *THE WRITER and her COMPANION stroll*
> *together, approaching the camera, the parcel carried*
> *under THE WRITER'S arm. The two characters*
> *walk purposefully in conversation though their words*
> *are inaudible until a cut to a close shot of their heads*
> *and upper bodies in sharp relief against the emerald*
> *hedges.*

THE WRITER *in response to a question:* Dark.
And there was too much smoke. I hate that foul
smell from the chemicals in those machines

THE COMPANION: It doesn't bother me.
I thought you'd be used to it by now.

Front on head and upper body shot as they walk.

THE WRITER: Just because I have to smell it all the time doesn't mean it becomes tolerable. Anyway we're busy with this now.
She indicates the box in her arms.

THE COMPANION: Where did you get it?

THE WRITER: That doesn't matter, it's too tiresome to go into and waste time on anyway.

THE COMPANION: what are we going to do with it?

THE WRITER: We should study it I suppose. Put it under scrutiny. I imagine if you look very closely at something, examine its fabric, one begins to see things that will illuminate a great deal. I seem to remember some promise of, through close study, one being able to behold historical events at a molecular level and by doing so see into the future.

THE COMPANION *after a few steps in silence and putting his hands in his pockets:* I don't follow you at all.

THE WRITER: Well let's take it to the examination room.

INT. EXAMINATION ROOM.
DAY OR NIGHT.

Shot of a door closing in an institutional corridor.
THE WRITER and her COMPANION sit
facing a one-way mirror through which they watch
the examination take place. Behind them stands
THE SUPERVISING TECHNICIAN
dressed in a lab coat. The shots cut between the
THE WRITER and her COMPANION in the
smaller supervision room behind the mirror and
the examination room proper where technicians work,
standing around a table. The box is carefully
opened, its lid hinged toward the camera. Light spills
from it illuminating the lab coat clad technician.
The contents however remain invisible while giving
the impression of being black, dense and disconcert-
ingly discarnate. Though they watch the work
the contents of the box remains as invisible to THE
WRITER and her COMPANION as it does to
the audience.

THE COMPANION *without turning to THE WRITER*: So let me get this straight. You have obtained this, and it remains unidentified? All you know about it is that it is contained in the cardboard box and wrapped in paper?

THE WRITER: Yes, but think about its possibilities.

THE COMPANION *with skepticism*: Hmmn. I don't feel inclined to speculate about something that seems so clearly plucked from some location and replaced in another where it palpably does not belong.

THE WRITER: Just wait.

> *Silence. THE COMPANION sings softly to himself*

THE SUPERVISING TECHNICIAN *to THE COMPANION*: What's that?

THE COMPANION *as if oblivious he has been making any sound at all*: Oh I don't know.

THE WRITER: Is something burning in here? There's a strange smell.

THE SUPERVISING TECHNICIAN: It could be wet paint. They said it was going to be painted again this week.

THE WRITER: No, it a burning smell not paint. I know what paint smells like.

THE SUPERVISING TECHNICIAN: The memo issued yesterday said the whole floor will be getting repainted during the next couple of weeks.

THE WRITER: It's not paint.

> *A technician enters the supervision room. She hands back the box, now wrapped in white poly-thene, with some accompanying documents to THE COMPANION who passes it directly to THE WRITER who, keeping hold of the box, passes the documents to THE SUPERVISING TECHNICIAN.*

THE TECHNICIAN: Here are the results.
She exits.

THE SUPERVISING TECHNICIAN *looking them over and then with some disbelief:* Ha. I don't really know what to say.

THE WRITER. What do you mean?

THE SUPERVISING TECHNICIAN: well, this has never happened before.
Again referring to the documents, turning them over and examining both sides.
Curious.

THE WRITER: I'm sorry, I don't understand.

THE SUPERVISING TECHNICIAN: I'm going to make a call.
He turns to the wall, lifts a wall mounted telephone receiver and dials.
Yes – Yes – I have them here – Well exactly – Yes.
Close shot of the heads of THE WRITER and her COMPANION. THE COMPANION looks weary.

Of course – Of course – I'll send them directly –
OK – OK good – Goodbye.

He replaces the receiver.

Well, I've arranged for you to see someone who
may be able to illuminate things a little. Take this.

*He scrawls a note on a scrap of paper and hands it
to THE WRITER as she rises.*

If you present this at the reception they will give
you directions.

They leave.

*EXT. GLASS FAÇADE OF A LARGE
BUILDING. A CITY. DAY*
People enter and exit through a revolving door.

*EXT. AN AFFLUENT RESIDENTIAL
STREET. A CITY. DAY*
*Arial shot of THE WRITER and her
COMPANION walking together. THE
WRITER carries the plastic wrapped box
under her arm.*

*EXT. OUTSIDE A LARGE, BLACK
FRONT DOOR. A CITY. EVENING*

Consulting a piece of paper THE COMPANION
*pushes a buzzer. Pause. At the sound of the lock
clicking open* THE COMPANION *looks to*
THE WRITER *and pushes open the door.*

*INT. A STONE STAIRWELL. A CITY.
EVENING*
THE WRITER *and her* COMPANION *climb
the stairs.*

*INT. IMPROVISED LECTURE THEATRE.
EVENING*
The door of the room opens and THE WRITER
and her COMPANION *are greeted by a man
in late middle age, graying, wearing a mustache.
Under his arm he carries a loaded slide carousel.
The room is a grand living room lit with a low
yellow light. The walls are lined with bookshelves
and two chairs positioned before a collapsable
projection screen.*

THE SCHOLAR *before* THE WRITER *and her*
COMPANION *can speak and without any introduction:* Welcome, welcome. Please take a seat. The
documentation and results got here an hour or so

ago so I think I'm more or less abreast of the situation. I'm going to ask you to indulge me before we make any real headway. Do take a seat.

He holds the crumpled documents in his fist and gestures with them towards the pair of chairs.

THE COMPANION *sitting:* Thank you.

THE SCHOLAR: Can I get you anything?
Idly he smoothes his mustaches in the mirror.

THE WRITER: No thank you.

THE SCHOLAR lowers the lights and activates a slide projector. Close shot of the carousel rotating to change the slide. Medium shot of THE WRITER and her COMPANION looking out towards the camera as if it were in the position of the screen on which the slides play. THE SCHOLAR stands behind them.

THE SCHOLAR: Are you comfortable? Let us begin.
He clicks the next slide into place.

In actual existence the moments of love are succeeded by the moments of satiety and sleep. The sincere remark is followed by a cynical distrust. Truth is fragmentary, at best: we love and betray each other in not quite the same breath but in two breaths that occur in fairly close sequence. But the fact that passion occurred in passing, that is then declined into a a more familiar sense of indifference, should not be regarded as proof of its inconsequence. And this is the very truth that drama wishes to bring us ...

> *During THE SCHOLAR's speech, various images are seen. It is unclear whether theses are slides that are shown to THE WRITER and her COMPANION or associative montage in the film's editing.*
> a) *A skeletal statuette.*
> b) *A lone empty Martini glass.*
> c) *A woman's face carved from a chunk of stone.*
> d) *Dirty dishes piled next to full ashtrays.*
> e) *Boxers sparring.*
> f) *Clouds of spinning strips of paper from a ticker-tape parade.*

Whether or not we admit it to ourselves, we are all haunted by a truly awful sense of impermanence. I have always had a particularly keen sense of this at cocktail parties, and perhaps this is the reason why I drink the Martinis almost as fast as I can snatch them from the tray. This sense is the febrile thing that hangs in the air. Horror of insincerity, of *not meaning*, overhangs these affairs like the cloud of cigarette smoke and the hectic chatter. This horror is the only thing, almost, that is left unsaid at such functions. All social functions involving a group of people not intimately known to each other are always under this shadow. They are almost always, in an unconscious way, like that last dinner of the condemned: where steak or turkey, whatever the doomed man wants, is served in his cell as a mockingly cruel reminder of what the great-big-little-transitory world had to offer ...

Pausing, his hand held over his mouth ponderously.

The audience can sit back in comforting dusk to watch a world which is flooded with light and in which emotion and actions have a dimension and dignity that they would likewise have in real existence, if only the shattering intrusion of time could be locked out[1].

> *THE WRITER and her COMPANION sit in silence, bewildered. A new slide clicks into place. Close shot of THE COMPANION's face bathed in light. THE SCHOLAR seems highly pleased and shuffles to his copious bookshelves. He returns with an armful of venerable looking tomes.*

THE SCHOLAR: Enough of my fables. These are bound to help. Excuse the pun.

> *THE WRITER and her COMPANION stand and he thrusts the books into THE COMPANION's arms.*

THE COMPANION *meekly:* Thank you.

THE SCHOLAR: Perhaps it's best if you take the other exit.

> *He leads them to another, smaller side door. They leave the room and are seen emerging into the grand gallery of a city museum. The museum is clearly*

closed and the lights are switched off. Paintings hang on the wall but what they depict is not visible in the low light. They seem black, foreboding. THE WRITER and her COMPANION look at each other in the moonlight spilling through the high windows. Exhaling THE COMPANION smiles incredulously and runs his fingers through his hair. THE WRITER smiles and looks at him. He breaks into a run and laughing she does the same. Wide shot of them running. The sound of their feet echos through the empty halls.

*end of reel 1

1   Tennessee Williams, *The Timeless World of A Play*,
     Author's foreword to *The Rose Tattoo*, 1951

Ohne Titel
2007
Tinte, Pumpsystem
Durchmesser 60 cm

In einem Park, zwischen Bäumen und
Büschen, zirkuliert in einer kreisrunden
Bodenmulde tiefschwarze Tinte. Die
Rotation erzeugt einen Strudel.

Ghost
2005
1-Kanal-Videoprojektion
8:00 Min.

Leere Blicke auf die verwaiste Villa
des Schriftstellers Curzio Malaparte
auf Capri. Der marode Zustand des
von ihm als Selbstporträt konzipierten
Hauses rückt ins Zentrum des Films ...
non plus d'histoire(s).

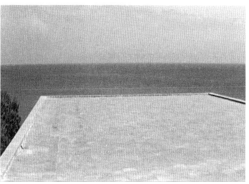

The Whirl
2007
12"-Vinylplatte, 1 Track
9:54 Min.

Ein Schallplattenobjekt und ein Hörstück
nach Edgar Allan Poes Kurzgeschichte
A Descent into the Maelstroem. Die Dinge,
die in der Erzählung von Poes Protago-
nisten nach einer Schiffshavarie in einem
wilden Strudel untergehen, erklingen, in
unterschiedlicher Reihenfolge, wiederholt,
als gesprochene Worte im Raum, während
sich das schwarze Vinyl auf dem Platten-
teller dreht.

*the man … the boat … the trunk …
the timber … the barrel … the boat…*

Beaufort
2004
1-Kanal-Videoprojektion
6:02 Min.

Beaufort ist eine Collage aus überarbeiteten
Filmsequenzen der Hollywood-Klassiker
Moby Dick (1956) und *Meuterei auf der Bounty*
(1962). In *Beaufort* verschmelzen die zwei
archetypischen Segelschiffe Pequod und
die Bounty zu ein und demselben Geister-
schiff, das ohne Besatzung über die Welt-
meere gleitet.

Folded Fog
2008
Piezoprint auf Papier
400 × 300 cm

Matthias Meyers komplexe Arbeiten kreisen
um die Grundstruktur, um die Bausteine
von populär-kultureller Narration sowie
ihrer Produktionsmechanismen: das Buch,
der Film, das Konzert, die Platte, der Text,
das Wort, der Buchstabe, das Klavier, das
Stück, die Note.

Indem Meyer ein per Animations-
programm erzeugtes Nebelbild (*Folded Fog*,
2008) als gefaltetes Poster in der Größe eines
Kinoplakats reproduziert, thematisiert er
ebenso die illusionistischen wie die ökono-
mischen Mechanismen der Traumfabriken
und spielt mit dem projizierten Begehren
ihrer Konsumenten. Indem Meyer aus den
Bildern wesentliche Handlungsmomente
entfernt, ihnen die eigentliche Story nimmt,
ist der Betrachter in der Lage, die so bloß-
gelegten Mechanismen der Produktion von
Narration und Illusion und ›Desire‹ zu sehen.

Stefan Kalmár

126

Index
2008
Selbstspielendes Klavier
Tonanalyse der *Mondscheinsonate*
von Ludwig van Beethoven (1801)

In *Index* wird Beethovens romantische
Mondscheinsonate (1801) durchdekliniert,
ein selbstspielendes Klavier ist so pro-
grammiert, dass es alle Töne der Reihe
nach aufsteigend sortiert spielt und der
am häufigsten vorkommende Ton derje-
nige ist, der zuletzt übrig bleibt.

Kissing a Cloud
2001
C-Print
43 × 35 cm

The Black Museum
2006
1-Kanal-Videoprojektion
4:52 Min.

The Black Museum basiert auf Szenen des
Dokumentarfilms *La Ville Louvre* (1990)
von Nicolas Philibert, welcher einen Blick
hinter die Kulissen des Pariser Museums-
betriebes wirft. Alle Gemälde, die im Film
auftauchen, wurden nachträglich komplett
eingeschwärzt. Das altehrwürdige Museum
wird hier selbst zum suprematistischen
Meisterwerk, geprägt von einer Ästhetik
der Negation, die aus der Absurdität un-
zähliger schwarzer Bilder ihr Potenzial
schöpft. Restauratoren, Kuratoren und andere Mitarbeiter behandeln jedes Bild wie
ein »Fenster zur Welt«, auch wenn dieses
für den Betrachter geschlossen bleibt.

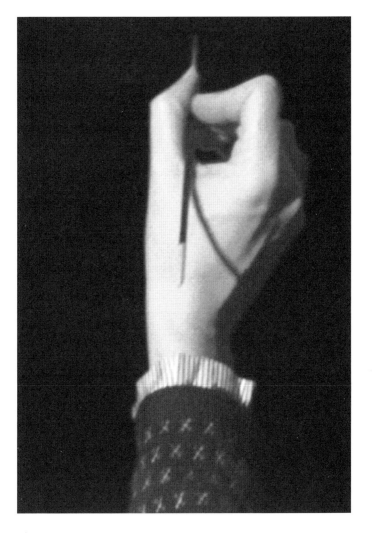

Caught Darkness
2005
C-Print
35 × 45 cm

Happy Ends
2001
Installation
Prima Kunst, Kiel

Ein fensterlos gebauter Ausstellungsraum:
an seiner Längsseite ein dunkler boden-
langer Vorhang, durch den man den Raum
betritt. An der Stirnseite eine kleine Licht-
öffnung oben in der Wand. Dahinter
ein unzugänglicher Nebenraum, aus dem
etwas Licht einfällt. Die Galerie erscheint
als bilderloses Kino, als düsterer Keller.

Anstatt einer Filmvorführung bildet
die diffuse Atmosphäre selbst das Ereignis.
Die Öffnungszeit liegt zwischen 20 und 22
Uhr. Es gibt ein Plakat, das auf die Ausstel-
lung hinweist. Die Informationen stehen
wie Untertitel auf der sonst schwarzen
Posterfläche. Auf der Rückseite ist ein Bild.
Es zeigt einen Blick auf eine unbekannte
Stadt bei Vollmond. Es ist das einzige Bild
der Ausstellung.

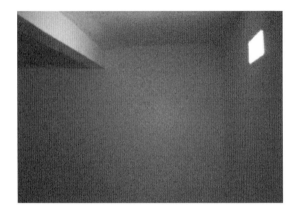

Double
2000
Performance
apexart, New York

Vom Schlüssel der Galerietür wird ein
Duplikat angefertigt und an einen in
New York tätigen Schauspieler übergeben.
Dieser erhält die Anweisung das Duplikat
im Stadtraum von Manhattan zu verlieren.
Weder im Ausstellungsraum, noch im
Außenbereich wird die Arbeit in dokumen-
tarischer Form sichtbar sein.

How can you smile when
you're deep in thought?
2009
20 Piezoprints auf Papier
je 27,5 × 32 cm

How can you smile when you're deep in thought?
ist die tonale Analyse eines Gesprächs-
mitschnittes zwischen Morton Feldman
und John Cage. Sie gibt den Sprach- und
Stimmklang der beiden Akteure wieder,
während sie sich über ihr Selbstverständnis
als Komponisten sowie über die Sinnfrage
künstlerischer Produktion unterhalten.
Die bildnerische Umsetzung in Form einer
Notenpartitur wird erweitert durch die
musikalische Interpretation der Notierung
mittels eines Vibraphones, dessen hohler,
metallischer Klang den Raum atmosphä-
risch füllt.

The Rising Snow/
The Falling Stars
2009
Buch, Hardcover, 164 Seiten
19,2 × 28,5 cm

Die Lesart von *The Rising Snow/The Falling Stars* funktioniert sowohl inhaltlich als auch formal in zwei Richtungen. Die beiden Buchdeckel sind mit jeweils unterschiedlichen Titeln versehen, die dasselbe Bildmaterial beschreiben. Im Inhalt tanzen, schweben und rieseln künstlich generierte Feinpartikel in filmischer Einzelbildabfolge über die Seiten.

Distanz oder Nähe lassen sich nicht erschließen. Der flüchtige Eindruck von Schneeflocken trifft auf ewige Konstellationen an einem möglichen Sternenhimmel.

THE
RISI
NG
SNO
W

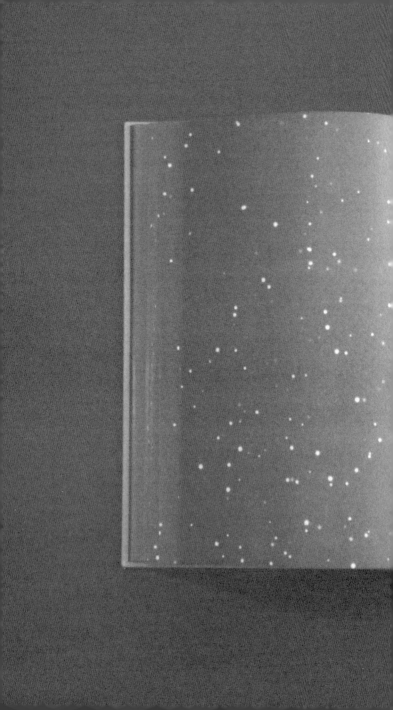

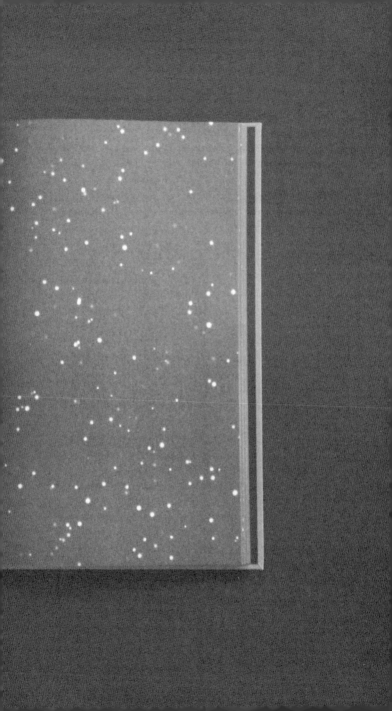

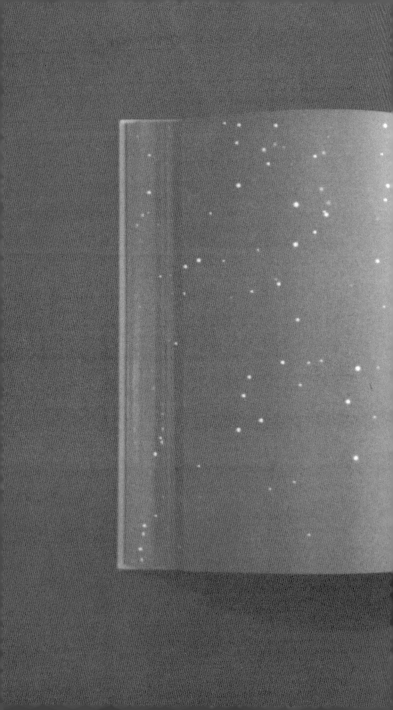

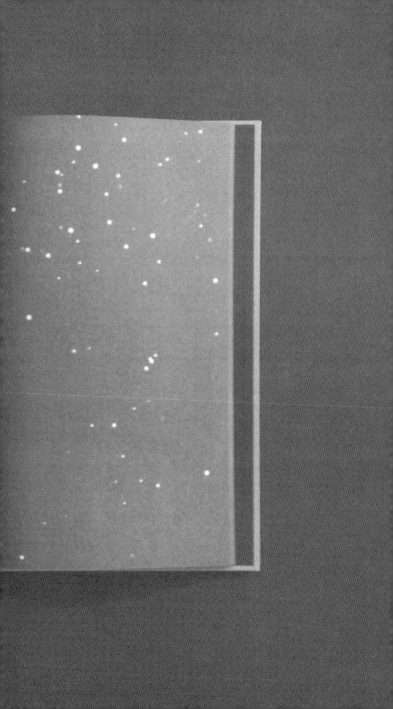

THE FALLING STARS

Smoke Archive
2010
C-Prints (Auswahl)
Größe variabel

Das *Smoke Archive* ist eine Sammlung
von Rauchdarstellungen in Spielfilmen.
Ein scheinbar chaotisches Archiv, das
sich in seiner Präsentationsform immer
wieder neu und anders zusammensetzt.

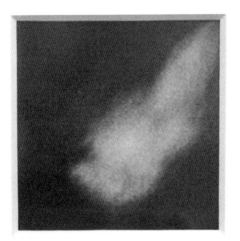

Empty Moon for an Empty Room
2005
1-Kanal-Videoprojektion
Projektionsgröße 1:1 zur
Originalkulisse, Loop

Das entleerte Bühnenbild aus Georges
Meliès' Film *Die Reise zum Mond* (1902) beleuchtet als unbeholfen holpernde Kulisse
den ansonsten leeren Ausstellungsraum.

Snowwww
2006
Offsetdruck auf Papier
32 × 24,5 cm

Das zentrale Motiv aus Michael Snows
Wavelength (1967) als Multiple, als stum-
mes Filmstill.

Sherwood (1. Staffel, Folgen 1–5)
2010
1-Kanal-Videoprojektion
14:53 Min.

Ein Streifzug durch das Dickicht der Film-
geschichte: Die Episoden von *Sherwood*
wagen sich auf das unwegsame Gelände von
Mythen und Legenden und entführen uns
in die unterschiedlichsten cineastischen Dar-
stellungen des sagenumwobenen Waldes.
Die Arbeit ist archivartig angelegt und be-
steht aus überarbeiteten Einstellungen der
großen Robin-Hood-Verfilmungen.

Abb. S. 5:

Ohne Titel (Le trou)
2009
Inkjet auf Papier, Rahmen
30 × 35 cm

Der einfache Eingriff in ein Filmstill aus
Jacques Beckers *Le trou* (1959). So wie das
Standfoto vor 50 Jahren dem Produktions-
ablauf des Films entnommen wurde, wird
hier, durch das Herausschneiden des
Sandes, die Zeit ein zweites Mal angehal-
ten. Das Loch, das sich mit seinen dahinter,
im Widerspruch liegenden Schattierungen
nicht so recht ins gegebene Bild einfügen
will, wird zum Mittelpunkt der Betrach-
tung. Von allen Seiten wird geschaut, und
wie nebenbei entsteht eine unerklärliche
Komplizenschaft aller beteiligten Personen.

Translations

–

Übersetzungen

What the Voice Can't See

1. The voice

»The voice is in the air.«
(Michel Chion, 1982)

In sound films, image and audio usually go hand in hand, appearing as two components that naturally belong together, with the sound perceived as an obedient shadow to the image. In contrast to voiceovers and music, synchronous sounds are readily absorbed by their accompanying image, and are wrongfully processed as redundant information. This appearance of utmost naturalness, which is in fact larger than life, is achieved with the help of any and all available tricks; it is a game whose goal it is to mask the effort that has gone into the synthesis of audio. The harder it is to detect any intervention, the more successful is the illusion.

In contrast, composer and filmmaker Michel Chion, who also writes for *Cahiers du Cinéma* and is the author of some of the most important monographs about sound in film, points out the arbitrary nature of the relationship between sound and image.

Robert Bresson compares discrete meetings of sound and image in cinema to chance acquaintances, while Michel Chion conducts a systematic analysis of the circumstances under which these meetings took place throughout the history of film in his »Audio-Vision«.[1] Instead of influencing each other in a harmonic way, these two modes of audio-visual perception, the visual and the audible, are locked in an agreement of reciprocity. Voice, central to sound film, is crucial in this relation.[2] Under this auspice, the history of film may be read as the history of image and sound approaching one another. Silent movies come from an age of innocence, unaffected by the apple of discord that is voice. In them, the preeminence of the visual accompanies the parallel devaluation of all other senses – *sight rules*. »Sound [...] withdraws into the shadows«, writes Walter Murch, film and sound editor for movies such as *The Conversation* and *Apocalypse Now* in his preface to »Audio-Vision«.[3]

The delay with which sound arrived on screen stands in stark contrast to human development, which proceeds from the sound continuum of prenatal darkness into the world of visual stimuli. According to Murch, cinema's formative years (1892–1927) were the exact opposite, spent in a hall of mirrors full of mute pictures. At that time, it was hard to predict that sound film would be more than just a phase of experimentation. Here is an example of the clear disdain with which an early moviegoer described a 1929 ›talkie‹: a »strange comedy in which the actors are closely miming in the lines with their mouths, while a mysterious ventriloquistic chorus leader, rigid and motionless [behind] the center of the screen … takes charge of the audible part of their silent speeches.«[4]

The possibilities opened by sound recording detach the object's »shadow« and let it exist in its own right. This is the birth of *musique concrète*. The ready availability of audiotape has encouraged experimentation ever since the 1950s. Once it is freed, sound can attach itself to anything, including the impossible. In the context of synchronous audio, image and sound form a relationship that is spontaneous, compelling and without any logical grounding – provided they occur at the exact same time. This ability to separate and mix is essential for sound film.

Therein, the voice of the not-yet-visible, internalized, absent body, the »acousmêtre«, occupies the most powerful position. Its

placelessness imbues it with a special omnipotence[5] exemplified by the ›voice that seeks a body‹: The entire history of cinema may be viewed from this perspective »as an endless movement of integrating the most disparate elements: sound and image, the sensory and the verbal.«[6]

In the context of Matthias Meyer's video works, one has to ask whether it is an intellectual faux pas to specifically address the subject of the voice. When something is systematically removed from a readily recognizable artifact at the visual level, may one ask what the sound layer held (or withheld) all this time – namely, for example, the sound itself?

Matthias Meyer works with material or selected sequences from feature film productions and art films that have long solidified their place within the cinema canon: Michelangelo Antonioni's *Blowup*, Méliès' *Voyage dans la Lune*, Chris Marker's *La Jetée*, Michael Snow's *Wavelength*, Jean-Luc Godard's *Le Mépris*, as well as *Mutiny on the Bounty* and *Moby Dick*. A well-known image, moving or still, elicits a clear memory of an inner image, perhaps with blurred edges or inconsistent details. What emerges can possibly displace other things, which remain invisible in this process. Meyer's films take apart everything that lends itself to dissection and work with omissions, each of which generates an effect of time travel, but at no point does voice come into play.

All finesses of synchronized sound (acousmatics, etc., as understood by Chion) play merely a supporting role in Matthias Meyer's films. Instead, his work focuses on the idea of image and sound lending themselves to separation and employs at most atmospheric audio or no sound at all, neither music nor human voice.

The question of sound (of the voice, of people) is examined in these videos by way of a double negation: As an immaterial representation of the body, in cinema, voice stands in immediate proximity to phenomena such as soul, shadow and doppelgangers, believed to survive physiological death. Where there is no sound, there is no voice; where there is no body, there is no immaterial representation.

A fair amount of fantasy is required to imagine the absent body that is yet to be united with its equally absent voice. The emptied room is the scene of a phantom dance.

Similarly, when one talks about sound along the lines of Chion and Murch, the vocabulary of negative space, sound vacuum and gaps, whose effect is to enrich meaning and thicken the atmosphere, soon enters the discourse. Murch sees the danger of contemporary cinema therein, that it crushes its objects with its range of mimetic and representative techniques. In contrast to other art forms, which are characterized by sensual limitation, film has matured into a medium of overstimulation.

With this in mind, we can view the history of image and sound in film as held together by two movements in the opposite direction. On the one hand, there are fantasies of unification and coming together, yearning to be fulfilled. However, it is more exciting to observe what, on the other hand, stands in the way of the fulfillment of this fantasy. »There is no place for completeness«: For Walter Murch, this characterizes the formation of Michel Chion's theory.[7]

2. The people

»No, this is not drama,
this is just change.«
(James Tenney, 1978)

I say, how heartless of you, man, to simply take the people out. I don't mean the soul, that there is no more soul in art – ›soul‹ is going a little too far for me, it's a bit too simplistic and overblown, – but the relationships between people, the exchanges that contain everything that the film tries to say. Don't tell me that you're not interested in the story that the film is telling; just trying to focus on the story takes everything out of you, it makes you crazy; that's why you won't read a book if you can help it, but you still expect a story for the price of a ticket, a story that every movie tells in one way or another; things and pictures and people and pictures people make of themselves and of things they surround themselves with, they all tell about their condition, and all this can't even be seen or has to be interpreted with great effort if of all the things that were in the movie, what you have at the end is just the Garden of Nature where the whole thing plays out with a load of vague, impersonal sound.

Right?

Also erased are narrative strategies and connotations in the widest sense of the word.

Try giving it subjectivity and see if it can retain it.

To fill the gaps that appear while the components of an arrangement reveal themselves as if of their own will.

A blacked-out painting is not simply a black painting (and it is certainly not a non-painting) without simultaneously not being a non-Malevich.

A person who doesn't talk isn't someone without a voice, a silent movie is something else entirely, while a film without sound is yet another thing.

If in doubt – leave it out.

What remains is an occasionally disillusioning drabness, but even the disillusionment isn't perfect.

The complete text of »À rebours« projected onto the screen letter by letter is not simply a difficult text, rendered practically unreadable, stretched to quadruple length of Andy Warhol's *Empire*.

[Internet Movie Database]: Warning: This synopsis is too short.

Instead, at this zero point of readability

As if a film's elements COULD BE added and subtracted from each other; of course, it's possible, at least from a technological perspective, but what is the product of the operation?

After all, eliminating meaning isn't an easy thing.

Unviewable works, undoing book burnings

Understood as a defense mechanism, magical processes taking place during acts of undoing result in the preceding action having never taken place; reverse action overrides the original action. This isn't how it works here.

To guarantee its success, magic demands perfection both from the process of creating an illusion and of disassembling it.

Matthias Meyer isn't interested in this. A determined non-reader, the artist appears as a weasel, a hare and a hedgehog, both of whom, of course, remaining invisible.

Some findings are thus phrased as conditionals: what would happen, if…? What would this be if this were the case?

Disillusion doesn't interest him. Same with the famous peek behind the scene, for example that of the Louvre – it remains hidden and borrows the scene's aura.

Something steps in to fill the gap. Disappearance, trickling away and a clear picture of the process.

The questions raised address the theme of perception more so than that of truth. Perception requires the viewer to assume a strenuous pose; sensory organs must perform yoga-like twists and turns.

Once a person is able to view himself as a compound subject (or one that is diffuse, but capable of taking on a compound form) and to similarly view sound in film as something separate from the body and having no necessary solid relationship to it, something that can be variously detached and reattached, again and again, at least with the aid of required and available apparatuses, and if this is seen not only as a threat, but also as a freedom, or if every perceived freedom is indeed seen as a threat and an uncertainty, but that it is also possible to desire uncertainty and not only wish to flee it like the devil from what he thinks is holy water, then it is possible to begin to play in these newly created spaces of combination and recombination. Matthias Meyer doesn't want to play. He opens these spaces and separates what lets itself be taken apart, but he never begins to play. He prefers to let the spaces stay empty. He likes having no one inside, and if there are ghosts, then only ghosts of ghosts, absent ghosts.

Besides being interested in apparatuses that enable certain phenomena (image, sound, subjectivity), usually on condition of their own imperceptibility, Matthias Meyer is obsessed with atmosphere. Apparatuses may become apparent when separable things are teased apart. But what about atmosphere? We can't let go of the idea. When two or more people talk about an atmosphere that existed somewhere, what are they talking about? It is a categorically undefined idea, and little effort has been made to clarify it;

a technical audio design concept; a gaseous envelope around a celestial body.

Metaphor could be a possible game, whose idea Walter Murch applies at the level of sound and whose introduction creates an open space for perception that resists cinema's »presence of everything«, preventing it from suffocating its object with its overabundance. Instead, an added value is made possible in reception. Quoting Aristotle, for Murch a metaphor means »naming a thing with that which is not its name« – here is yet another beautiful phantom dance.

3. No one

»Every place has its
own silence.«
(Michel Chion, 1991)

(Empty Moon for an empty Room) No one lands on the moon. This creates a flickering, rattling image. The earth does not rise on the horizon, plunging the scene into an otherworldly light. This landscape dotted with craters appears whole and indivisible, but one half of it must nonetheless disappear behind the other.

This is a place that no human being has seen, not Georges Méliès, not anyone else, and not just up to this time, but even now, in 1902; this image is a product

of magic. The unseen image, a picture of the unseen. These are journeys in time, into film's other time layers. Travel through cineastic time, the chronology of film history. What, then, is a location? A place where action takes place.

(Untitled) He doesn't walk up the steps to climb the slope leading to the crime scene, at first like a shadow, then emerging from the green into the hazy skies; it is impossible to say whether it has already rained or is only about to. The trees rustle. Just before he reaches the top, he doesn't hurry his step, doesn't scale two steps at a time and turn left, where a seemingly endless picket fence encircles the wide Maryon Park meadow.

He does not look down to adjust the camera lodged between his hands, and he doesn't walk off into the expanse of the field from the left under the heaving foliage hanging from the branches. He doesn't settle into a swift stride and turn around, to see if someone is coming, and there is no trace of intense purposefulness on his face. There is no searching glance, no patting his surroundings, no ducking behind the bushes in the middle of the neatly mowed clearing. No one came here for no reason at all, the camera rests on the ground, resigned, two lonely branches gently stroke his hair and shoulders, eyes pointed skyward, scanning the rustling treetops.

All the time he believed to have found evidence of something in the pictures. A system of evidences. He has an eye, he has learned the science of examining with his sight, it is his profession. A face behind the fence. A face is comprised of white dots, and it disintegrates back into them again. The woman has something in her eyes that appears to give him clues. Something between the frames.

The hardly perceptible loop underscores the microrhythmic dynamics of nature in London's Maryon Park. To go with these »microrhythms«, Michel Chion conceived quick movements on the screen created by snow, smoke, rain, rippling surfaces of water or sand and film grain. [8] These elements summate to fast, fluid rhythms, which fill the image with a vibrating temporarity: »It is as if this technique affirms a kind of time proper to sound cinema as a recording of the microstructure of the present.«

Untitled returns to the point in time where sound film transformed cinema into time-art, and acts out its chronographic substance. Synchronized sound influences the perception of time inside the image. With sound, it became necessary for film to stabilize its projection speed. Film is »written in time«. [9]

Sound affects the irreversibility of image succession and of time, and it does so for every single falling drop of water (each a story in its own right).

Music itself brings in a dimension of real time and linearity. Consider the piano: each note begins to die the minute it is born, this is real time governed by indices; the sound of speech, however, takes elasticity out of time, and everyday chronology returns to the screen.

Conversely, in *Untitled* time is not yet or is no longer vectorized.

It shall be nullified, all that is an occurrence. Instead of conveying time in a directional trajectory, the natural processes in Maryon Park appear rather in the sense of »anemphatic music« as understood by Chion, continuing, untouched by the action, as a reflection of the mechanical nature of film and its unwinding; in turn, the film itself emphatically tries to make us forget this fact. [10]

In narrative film, sound has a unifying effect on the image by helping bridge visual gaps and providing an atmospheric envelope, »a framework that seems to contain the image, a ›heard space‹ in which the ›seen‹ bathes«. [11] If there are gaps that are not spanned by sound, the envelope is left open. For example, a jump cut can connect two spaces in a paradoxical way with the help of a subjective figure; if this figure is omitted, as in *Untitled*, the spaces fall apart and revert into themselves. What is happening here? Perhaps it is a turnaround of the phantasm of a hard reverse shot, the idea that the character could see us just like we saw him before, that our space as viewers is now being emptied? A wide-reaching clearing of space…

The audible chirping of the birds is a synonym for what one would like to hear, for you are in fact listening, but there is nothing, no one is harkening for clues, there is nothing but the chirping bird and incessant wind which no one and nothing is capable of assigning to precise coordinates in space.

(*Beaufort*) No one hangs in the ropes. No one is being beaten. Blows would be accompanied by sounds, which help convince ourselves of them. No one is staging a mutiny below deck, in the belly of the ship. No one is sailing the seven seas. No 5 000 natives from six South Sea islands are part of an unusual cast. Interiors, exteriors, all at the same distance. No teleporter mediates between these stages. (That would have been the person).

Someone has to be there. (Someone with a camera). (Let's try to close the gap). A ship is an island. It is a world of dead things, in disuse. Taken alone, it is senseless and without sound. The lamp swinging above the ship's maps would normally be a silent image in a sound film. Of course, this »silence« must be created using audio technology, silence is a moment of resonance, embedded in a continuous background

soundtrack (of the sea, gulls, fish). A silent film, to which time has not yet been introduced. Or, it's as if nothing happened after the removal of time. Someone sees this. There is no indication of the nature, cause or time of the loss.

No battles have taken place, or if they did, it was a long time ago. These are images of a careful inspection, which point to an questionable context (deemed long lost and found, perhaps decades later, in a rusty film tin in the basement of a South American theater); in other words, they raise the very question of context.

(*Ghost*) Wearing a suit, his left hand lodged in his pant pocket like an actor in a movie, he doesn't go through the bushes that push through the rocks, still green, even though they sit under the merciless sun. He wouldn't need to free his hands even when descending from dizzying heights.

He does not now make his way in the other direction along the switchback framed by walls that cut through the thousand-year-old landscape. Not he, nor anyone else who would find himself in his company, casual and donning the same light summer garb, following the sudden turn of the road and entering the realm of shadows where the mercilessness of the sun becomes suddenly comprehensible in the cool and darkness below the canopy of trees.

Much becomes apparent in the light of day and through the vulnerability of the eye.

»In the cinema, to look is to explore, at once spatially and temporally, in a ›given-to-see‹ (field of vision) that has limits contained by the screen. But […] the aural field is much less limited or confined, its contours uncertain and changing.« [12]

Just then he would have realized that he would have liked to have shielded his eyes, he would have liked to have worn sunglasses – if he had had a pair, had he thought of it.

Like a stone armadillo, the house sits high above the water, unapproachable from three sides, accessible from the fourth.

The roof is not a roof, but a roof and stairs in one, his head and shoulders aren't a head and shoulders in flights of stairs, no clear divide between the stairs and roof, their functions blurring into each other form this angle.

No one says: Schöne gelbe Farbe. No one returns: Danke.

No one walks through the frame. All this time waves break on cliffs and washed-out cries of seagulls assail the ears. No one walks across the roof. But I seem to hear footsteps. Someone could be walking on the roof, descending the cliff, sitting at this window. In a different time. The fizz of the sea gets louder. With its sound, even the borders of this space that lie outside the frame are defined as belonging to this world, being here. The places, which the figures must occupy, are solidly affixed to the coordinates defined by the buildings. The atmosphere creates a space with an unnamed depth, 'somehow synthetic, artificial. Instead of defining this space, it acts as the space itself.

(*The Black Museum*) Paintings are blackened, removed and taken away. There are people, but no sound. Silence movie? Silent film? They don't talk. Because the film itself is highly visual, there must be two types of images here, giving rise to a buoyant atmosphere. Conservators are touching up black. The artists' doppelgangers, what are they scheming, the way they are consumed with the fine details of black? In cinema, an image is a frame, and a feature-length movie contains hundreds of shots and tens of thousands of stills. A film »image« does not signify content, but rather a container, and may therefore be empty, black. When a black image remains black, it is not an absence or a nothing, but is a rectangle, filled-in and presently visible to the viewer. The frame affirms itself as a fundamental container which remains after the picture is gone, a dimension of the black picture that is maintained to some degree by end credits. [13] At one point in *The Black Museum*, museum workers stretch a giant black canvas like a curtain or a carpet across the entire screen, touching the frame's outer edges, comic-like guarantors that the action is moving forward, and image and frame become one and the same, producing an occasion for amusement.

(*No Empire*) Empire – the word alone projects the grand image of Andy Warhol's view, cleared of the Empire State Building, and additionally signifies this sensual realm on the screen as well as the limits of this realm. Which limits could these be?

The night sky, the flickering gray, the black overhead. That, which surrounds the Earth – atmosphere. When a film tries to present a non-objective subject per se, its materiality and figurative description unexpectedly combine into the idea of atmosphere.

In this realm, as in a universe inhabited by spirits, absence and presence are no longer contradictions. And as long as we are on the subject of ghosts: Some appear blurry, while others are best captured without any focus.

4. Look at these images in focus!

Again I am looking at fog pushing past my windows, smoke or snow drifts, things whose origins aren't clear to me and whose names I do not know; yet again my so-called studies lead

me to the shadow, detached from the body, and to the relationship between image and sound. What would be, if there were people?

Something is holding me back, I cannot call it by its name.

An overlay of exposed stills from Chris Marker's experimental film *La Jetée*, which is told almost continuously using photographic images, can be seen in Matthias Meyer's print *A Museum of Its Memory*. Here, all of the film's images are reduced to one. Of course, this isn't readily apparent. What is visible is gray, depicting nothing, a blurry pictorial space of an uncertain origin.

When looking at *Folded Fog*, a 3 by 4 meter computer-generated grisaille, whose other notable characteristic is that it can be folded, echoes of the aesthetic tradition of blurring objects that goes back to before the turn of the 20th century cannot be missed. Ways of looking at landscape, borrowed from painting and transferred to the medium of photography are accompanied by a large dose of poeticism as well as appreciation of art theory applied to phenomena such as fog, moonlight and twilight. According to Wolfgang Ullrich, fog with its »natural blur« released the scope of representation from the depicted object, allowing it to become independent of the subject. [14] In step with contemporary atmospheric requirements, which correspond with a dismissal of objects' materiality, blurry photography negates the objects' plasticity, including the three-dimensionality of the space itself using over- and underexposure, turning these into pure atmospherical space. To create this effect, objects still in focus, parts of objects or contrasts must be present within the disappearing space, preceding its disappearance. Free of such residues, Matthias Meyer's blurry images do not create such atmospheric spaces, and it is their own, usually hidden materiality that they reference. Still, it would be absurd to completely separate the subjects of *Folded Fog*, *No Empire* and *A Museum of Its Memory* from the aesthetic of blurry photography which relates a glance into the distance, »beholding everything and nothing« with the goal of »finding oneself in the picture«.[15] It is, however, more important that the romantic, antimodern stance which takes shape in this tradition is returned to its rightful position in being transported to the age of silent film, as when Georges Méliès' moon is cleared of its human visitors in *Empty Moon for an Empty Room* to remind us that there was once a time in the history of film when it was possible to fulfill the great pipe dream of actually entering the picture. Here, the promises made by the possibilities opened by film are revisited.

The blur of symbolist painting, calling up hidden, truer worlds;[16] the particular forces of the medium which in its early phase let the photographic image appear as a product of special magic, and therefore made it the preferred medium for communication with ghosts. The dimension of the occult certainly resonates – just as the concept of the voice of the dead is associated with the early days of the telephone and the gramophone – in Matthias Meyer's blur phenomena. The question of perception, however, plays a much bigger role than that of truth.

What is missing from the foreground of *Folded Fog* is a Caspar David Friedrich-like figure seen from the back, acting as a mediator of the image space: There he is again, not. These images may be approached only from the perspective of their history and tradition, so that it is clear what one sees and what one does not. So it comes that even works such as *No Empire*, where the Empire State Building has been thoroughly removed from Andy Warhol's already extremely pared-down *Empire*, and *A Museum of Its Memory* reference the pure source of their own materiality, still carrying traces of their concrete representation.

Traditional blurred photography, whether recreating inner images[17] or offering a boundless view to an all-seeing eye, measures its subjects against the scale of an

213

aesthetic autonomy. In contrast, Matthias Meyer's unfocused and empty spaces, which appear to simultaneously release and swallow the representational, subjective, speaking world, necessarily summon contexts in order to embed themselves into these.

5. Postscript:
A conceivably clear image

It can be added that by reusing distinct motifs, which combine into an erratic »body of work«, a list of subjects, which appear and disappear, all the while passing through or foundering away, a conceivably clear image is produced. The title *The rising snow / The falling stars* speaks of this double movement. Here, the voice is examined in this sence: Formulated as a question (»How can you smile when you're deep in thought?«) that Morton Feldman and John Cage discussed in a radio program in 1966, the voice disappears at the moment of its visualization. The discussion between Feldman and Cage about the value of the idea in artistic work and, consequently, the concept of the artist and that of the idea is transferred by Matthias Meyer into a pure musical sound of spoken melodies of the artists' voices played on a vibraphone, additionally recorded in written form as a score. The voice is discreetly cancelled by

the music in a manifold reversal of the relationships between notation and execution, concept and performance.

In turn, *Index*, a self-playing piano installed together with a large-scale screen projection of *Folded Fog*, does *not* play Beethoven's *Moonlight Sonata*. On the contrary, it reproduces the acoustical inventory, slowly and according to a specific arithmetical key. These are the image and sound of no existing movie. Fog and screen on the one hand, and the piano in an emphatic, perhaps Loriot-like sense on the other, illustrate the traditional concept of aura at the very moment of its loss.

In a park corner, a small swirl of black ink: a black hole, which continually swallows and simultaneously regenerates itself. Reminiscence of a vinyl recording titled *The Whirl:* There lies the spiraling course of grooves on the black disc, turning in perfect correspondence with the enumeration of all the doomed objects caught inside the ceaselessly raging whirlpool of Edgar Allan Poe's »Maelstrom«.

(Translation: Alice Bayandin)

214

1   See Michel Chion, *Audio-Vision: Sound on Screen*,
    pub. and trans. by Claudia Gorbman, introduc-
    tion by Walter Murch. New York 1994.
    [Fr. *L'audio-vision* 1991]
2   Michel Chion, *The Voice in Cinema*, pub. and
    trans. by Claudia Gorbman. New York 1999.
    [Fr. *La voix au cinéma* 1982]
3   See Walter Murch, intr. to *Audio-Vision: Sound
    on Screen*, a. a. O., pg. viii.
4   Chion, *The Voice in Cinema*, pg. 131
5   Chion, *The Voice in Cinema*, pg. 24: »The
    one you don't see is in the best position to
    see you.« Due to its panoptic omnipotence,
    »acousmêtre« often accompanies a paranoid,
    even obsessive fantasy. Michel Chion talks of
    the ›all-seeing voice‹.
6   Chion, *Audio-Vision: Sound on Screen*, pg. 183
7   Murch, *Audio-Vision: Sound on Screen*, pg. xxiv
8   Chion, *Audio-Vision: Sound on Screen*, pg. 16
9   Chion, *Audio-Vision: Sound on Screen*, pg. 17
10 Chion, *Audio-Vision: Sound on Screen*, pg. 9
11 Chion, *Audio-Vision: Sound on Screen*, pg. 47
12 Chion, *Audio-Vision: Sound on Screen*, pg. 33
13 See Chion, *Audio-Vision: Sound on Screen*, 66f.
14 See Wolfgang Ullrich, *Die Geschichte der
    Unschärfe*. Berlin 2002, 2009. Here, pg. 19
15 See Ullrich, *Die Geschichte der Unschärfe*, pg. 42
16 See Ullrich, *Die Geschichte der Unschärfe*, pg. 48f.
17 See Ullrich, *Die Geschichte der Unschärfe*, pg. 98

Kein Verlangen nach leuchtenden Farben

Ein unvollständiges Drehbuch

Die Leinwand bleibt für einige Sekunden dunkel, bis ein mechanisches Klicken zu hören ist.

Detailaufnahme eines Tonabnehmers, der über einer sich drehenden Schallplatte schwebt. Das Surren des Antriebsriemens ist zu hören. Ein zweites Klicken, und die Nadel senkt sich. Nach dem typischen Knistern beginnt die Musik. Giuseppe Di Stefano singt »Una Furtiva Lagrima«. Ein plötzlicher Stimmungswechsel als die Zeilen des Vorspanns über schnell montierten Bildern aus unterschiedlichen Zeiten und von unterschiedlichen Orten erscheinen. Eine leere Fläche aus Kork. Hände tauchen vor der Kamera auf und heften ein dunkles Foto an die Pinnwand. Die Daumen geben das Bild frei, aber die Einstellung endet, bevor das Motiv zu erkennen ist. Eine Zange bewegt Fotografien in chemischen Flüssigkeiten, die Leinwand ist vom tiefroten Licht der Dunkelkammer überflutet. Nahaufnahmen der Kräuselungen und des Lichtspiels auf der roten Flüssigkeit. Schnelle Kamerafahrt über lange Bücherregale, die Buchtitel sind nicht zu entziffern, die Kamera wird langsamer und fährt über die abgenutzten bunten Buchrücken. Sie schwenkt zu einem Schreibtisch, auf dem sich ein Revolver mit kurzem Lauf, Näpfe mit Wasserfarben und eine nicht ganz scharfe, gerahmte Porträtaufnahme befinden. Eine Frau faltet sorgfältig schwarze und graue Stoffbahnen. Nahaufnahmen von verblichenem, verfallenem Gips, einem Punkt, ein Pinsel wird in Wasser herumgewirbelt, ein getrocknetes Buchenblatt als Lesezeichen benutzt, Sahneschwaden in einer Tasse mit schwarzem Kaffee. Die Umrisse eines Paares, das am Strand spaziert, im Gegenlicht der auf- oder untergehenden Sonne. Milch sprudelt über den Rand eines Glases, in das mit einem Strohhalm hineingeblasen wird. Wieder der Plattenspieler, die Nadel ist in der Mitte der Spur angekommen. Die Musik wird ausgeblendet.

INNEN. DIE WOHNUNG DER AUTORIN. EINE EUROPÄISCHE STADT. ABEND

Man hört die Stimme einer Frau. Während sie spricht: Die Kamera

fährt ganz nah an einem orange-
farbigem Pentel-Stift aus Plastik
entlang, der auf einer hölzernen
Schreibtischoberfläche liegt.
Ähnliche Nahaufnahmen von un-
liniertem Schreibpapier und
Notizbuchseiten. Karos, Linien,
rote Randleisten. Die weitere
Ausstattung des Schreibtisches wird
von der Kamera erkundet. Ein
Glas Wasser, ringförmige Kaffee-
flecken auf einem fotokopierten
Dokument, ein Paar orangefarbige
Plastikstifte der gleichen Marke
wie zuvor, zusammengehalten mit
einem Gummiband, Büroklam-
mern, verbogene Heftklammern.

DIE AUTORIN *off:* Ich habe mit
diesem Stift gerungen, weil er sich
so gut in meiner Hand anfühlt.
Wenn er zum Ende dessen kommt,
was auch immer ich geschrieben
habe, muss ich ihn auf den Schreib
tisch zurücklegen und mich der
Verantwortung für das stellen, was
ich zu Papier gebracht habe.
Während ich schreibe mag ich
ihn nicht ablegen, weil ich fürchte,
der Zauber könnte gebrochen
werden. Ich nehme ihn mit, wenn
ich eine Kaffeepause mache oder
zur Toilette gehe. Ich sitze dort
und rolle ihn zwischen meinen
Fingern, bis es an der Zeit ist, wieder an die Arbeit zu gehen. In
Momenten, in denen ich unter besonders hohem Druck stehe oder
in akute Unruhe verfalle, habe ich
immer einen Reservestift in der
Brusttasche meiner Bluse, sodass

ich denjenigen, mit dem ich schreibe, falls er austrocknet sofort er-
setzen kann, ohne in einer Schub-
lade kramen oder in den Taschen
des auf dem Küchentisch abgeleg-
ten Mantels danach suchen zu
müssen. Also werde ich von ihm
tyrannisiert und bin gleichzeitig
von ihm abhängig, so als wäre er
ein Kuscheltuch. Ja, dies alles
drückt ein tiefes Misstrauen gegenüber meinem Textverarbeitungs-
programm aus, das so ganz
ungenutzt bleibt wie ein über-
flüssiges, aus Pflichtbewusstsein
übernommenes Erbstück. Durch
diesen Stift also, und durch das
Arsenal seiner Brüder in meiner
Brusttasche oder im Schreibwa-
rengeschäft, spüre ich die Gewiss-
heit, dass ich überhaupt in der
Lage bin zu schreiben. Ich habe
lange geforscht, bevor ich mich
auf diese spezielle Marke verlegt
habe, um sicherzugehen, dass
die Tinte so haltbar ist, dass egal
wie viele Getränke ich über dem
Manuskript verschütte, es nicht
verwischt. Auch können sich
die Wörter nicht auf mysteriöse
Weise im Äther verteilen, wie sie
es täten, wenn der Computer ab-
stürzt oder sein Stromkabel ver-
sehentlich aus der Wand gezogen
wird. Aber diese absurde Ablehnung ist nur ein Mittel zum Zweck,
zwei Charaktere vorzustellen,
die in dieser Familie von Stiften
geboren und dem Papier anver-
traut wurden. Eine ihrer bemer-
kenswerten Eigenschaften ist ihre

Fähigkeit, nach Belieben Raum und Zeit zu durchqueren, ohne Rücksicht auf Entfernung oder Richtung. Ob das mit ihrem Einverständnis geschieht oder nicht, bleibt unklar, aber es geschieht dennoch. Hier sehen wir sie.

AUSSEN. BAHNHOF.
EINE ANDERE STADT.
NACHT
Totale auf ein Paar, einen Mann und eine Frau als bloße Silhouetten, die sich Arm in Arm von der Kamera entfernen. Sie werden vom Licht der Straßenlaternen hinterfangen, das durch die Bogengänge neben der Fahrbahn fällt. Wölkchen von Rauch oder Nebel. Ein Zoom-out zeigt ein weiteres Paar, das auf einer Bank sitzt und das erste Paar aus der Entfernung beobachtet. Dieses Paar erhebt sich und geht, ins Gespräch vertieft, fort. Die Kamera folgt, um zu zeigen, dass sich diese beiden in einem Filmset befinden. Sie verlassen die künstlich verdunkelte Halle, steigen vorsichtig über Kabel und schlängeln sich durch die Crew. Sie laufen in blendendes Tageslicht und lassen die arbeitenden Techniker zurück, während Nebel aus Maschinen wabert, den Ventilatoren überall verteilen. Die Kamera, eindeutig Teil dieses Studios, erhebt sich an einem mechanischen Kran, um eine Vogelperspektive einzunehmen. Die Beleuchtung erzeugt eine Illusion von Schwarz-Weiß-Film.

Die Figur links bin ich, und die andere ist, nun ja, jemand anderes.

Die Musik ertönt erneut, und eine zweite Serie von Bildern beginnt. Halbtotale Fahrt über einen Tisch in einem holzvertäfelten Konferenzraum, an dem Gelehrte sitzen. Sie treten lebhaft gestikulierend auf, diskutieren einen Gegenstand, der sich links außerhalb des Bildes befindet. Totale eines Büros, in dem Angestellte eifrig arbeiten. Nahaufnahme zweier Personen, die etwas auf einem Computerbildschirm diskutieren, das von ihren Köpfen verdeckt wird. Eine Einstellung aus der offenbar abgeschlossenen Umgebung eines Labors. Laboranten bearbeiten etwas, indem sie ihre Arme durch Löcher in den Wänden in dort befestigte, spezielle Gummihandschuhe stecken. Der Gegenstand ihrer Aufmerksamkeit ist fast ganz außerhalb des Bildes. Was es auch sein mag, es erscheint schwarz, unheimlich und seltsam unfassbar. Großaufnahme von außerhalb der abgeschlossenen Umgebung auf einen arbeitenden Laboranten mit seinen Armen bis zu den Ellbogen in den Löchern. Die Musik klingt ab.

INNEN. U-BAHN.
TAG ODER NACHT
DIE AUTORIN und ihr BEGLEITER sitzen beieinander. Zwei oder drei andere Fahrgäste sind im Waggon.

DIE AUTORIN *off*: Es wird deutlich, dass sie Gefährten sind, aber nicht unbedingt Liebende.

DER BEGLEITER: Was ist das?
Er zeigt auf eine Schachtel, die die Autorin auf dem Schoß hält.

DIE AUTORIN: Das ist eine Schachtel.
Sie untersucht sie.
Sie ist in braunes Papier eingeschlagen, und ich glaube, sie ist aus Pappe.
Versuchsweise klopft sie darauf.

DER BEGLEITER: Hattest du sie schon beim Einsteigen?

DIE AUTORIN *unaufmerksam*: Hmm.

DER BEGLEITER: Was ist drin?

DIE AUTORIN: Ich weiß es nicht.

AUSSEN. EIN WOLKEN-LOSER BLAUER HIMMEL. TAG
Vogelstimmen.

AUSSEN. EIN PARK. TAG
DIE AUTORIN und ihr BEGLEITER spazieren auf die Kamera zu, das Päckchen unter dem Arm DER AUTORIN. Die beiden wirken zielbewusst und sind in eine Unterhaltung vertieft, doch

ihre Stimmen sind nicht zu hören, bis zum Schnitt zu einer Nahaufnahme mit ihren Köpfen und Oberkörpern als scharfes Relief vor einer smaragdgrünen Hecke.

DIE AUTORIN *beantwortet eine Frage*: Dunkel. Und es gab zu viel Rauch. Ich hasse diesen fauligen Geruch der Chemikalien in diesen Maschinen.

DER BEGLEITER: Das stört mich nicht. Ich dachte, du hättest dich inzwischen daran gewöhnt.

Frontal auf Gesicht und Oberkörper, während sie weitergehen.

DIE AUTORIN: Dass ich es die ganze Zeit riechen muss, heißt nicht, dass es erträglicher wird. Wie auch immer, im Moment müssen wir uns hierum kümmern.
Sie zeigt auf die Schachtel unter ihrem Arm.

DER BEGLEITER: Wo hast du es her?

DIE AUTORIN: Das spielt keine Rolle. Es ist zu lästig, jetzt darauf einzugehen und es wäre sowieso reine Zeitverschwendung.

DER BEGLEITER: Was stellen wir damit an?

DIE AUTORIN: Ich schlage vor, es zu untersuchen, es einer genauen Prüfung zu unterziehen.

Ich stelle mir vor, dass wenn man etwas ganz genau betrachtet und seine Struktur untersucht, Dinge zum Vorschein kommen, die eine Menge erklären können. Ich meine mich an eine Art Versprechen zu erinnern, welches besagt, dass man – durch genaues Studium – historische Ereignisse auf einer molekularen Ebene betrachten und auf diese Weise die Zukunft vorhersehen sehen kann.

DER BEGLEITER, *nachdem er einige Schritte lang geschwiegen hat, mit den Händen in den Taschen:* Ich kann dir nicht folgen.

DIE AUTORIN: Gut, bringen wir es in den Untersuchungsraum.

*INNEN.
UNTERSUCHUNGSRAUM.
TAG ODER NACHT*

Aufnahme einer sich schließenden Tür im Flur einer Einrichtung. DIE AUTORIN und ihr BEGLEITER sitzen gegenüber eines Einwegspiegels, durch den sie die Untersuchung beobachten. Hinter ihnen steht DER TECHNISCHE LEITER DES LABORS, bekleidet mit einem Laborkittel. Die Einstellungen wechseln zwischen DER AUTORIN und ihrem BEGLEITER im kleineren Zuschauerraum und dem eigentlichen Labor, in dem

Technische Assistenten an einem Tisch stehen und arbeiten. Die Schachtel wird vorsichtig geöffnet, ihr Deckel Richtung Kamera aufgeklappt. Licht dringt heraus und beleuchtet die Laborarbeiter in ihren Kitteln. Der Inhalt bleibt allerdings unsichtbar, während der Eindruck von etwas Schwarzem, Dichtem und beunruhigend Immateriellen entsteht. Obwohl sie der Untersuchung zusehen, bleibt der Inhalt der Schachtel für DIE AUTORIN *und ihren* BEGLEITER *ebenso unsichtbar wie für die Zuschauer.*

DER BEGLEITER, *ohne sich* DER AUTORIN *zuzuwenden:* Nur um es zu verstehen: Du hast das hier bekommen, und es ist noch nicht identifiziert? Alles was du darüber weißt, ist, dass es sich in der Pappschachtel befindet und in Papier eingeschlagen ist?

DIE AUTORIN: Ja, aber ich denke über seine Möglichkeiten nach.

DER BEGLEITER *skeptisch:* Hmm. Ich bin nicht geneigt, über etwas zu spekulieren, das so eindeutig irgendeinem Ort entnommen wurde, um an einem anderen platziert zu werden, wo es offensichtlich nicht hingehört.

DIE AUTORIN: Warte ab.

Stille. DER BEGLEITER *singt leise vor sich hin.*

DER TECHNISCHE LEITER
DES LABORS *zum BEGLEITER:*
Was ist das?

DER BEGLEITER, *als wäre er sich
nicht bewusst, überhaupt ein Geräusch
gemacht zu haben:* Oh, ich weiß es
nicht.

DIE AUTORIN: Brennt es hier
drinnen? Es riecht seltsam.

DER TECHNISCHE LEITER
DES LABORS: Es könnte frische
Farbe sein. Es hieß, diese Woche
würde wieder neu gestrichen.

DIE AUTORIN: Nein, es riecht
verbrannt, nicht nach Farbe.
Ich weiß, wie Farbe riecht.

DER TECHNISCHE LEITER
DES LABORS: Im gestrigen
Memo wurde mitgeteilt, dass der
ganze Flur in den nächsten zwei
Wochen neu gestrichen würde.

DIE AUTORIN: Das ist nicht
Farbe.

*Eine Laborantin betritt den Zu-
schauerraum. Sie gibt die Schachtel,
die jetzt in Klarsichtfolie gewickelt
ist, zurück und händigt DEM
BEGLEITER einige zugehörige
Dokumente aus, welche er direkt
DER AUTORIN gibt,
die – weil sie die Schachtel hält –
diese ihrerseits an DEN
TECHNISCHEN LEITER
DES LABORS weiterreicht.*

DIE LABORANTIN: Hier sind
die Ergebnisse.
Sie verlässt den Raum.

DER TECHNISCHE LEITER
DES LABORS, *die Dokumente
überfliegend und dann mit einigen
Zweifeln:* Ha! Ich weiß wirklich
nicht, was ich sagen soll.

DIE AUTORIN: Wie meinen
Sie das?

DER TECHNISCHE LEITER
DES LABORS: Also, so etwas ist
noch nie passiert.
*Weist wieder auf die Dokumente,
wendet sie und betrachtet Vorder-
und Rückseiten.
Merkwürdig.*

DIE AUTORIN: Es tut mir leid,
ich verstehe nicht.

DER TECHNISCHE LEITER
DES LABORS: Ich muss
telefonieren.
*Er dreht sich zur Wand, hebt ein
dort angebrachtes Telefon ab und
wählt eine Nummer.*
Ja – Ja – Ich habe sie hier – Genau –
Ja.
*Nahaufnahmen der Gesichter
DER AUTORIN und ihres
BEGLEITERS. DER
BEGLEITER sieht müde aus.*
Natürlich – Natürlich –
Ich schicke sie Ihnen sofort –
Okay – Okay, gut –
Auf Wiederhören!
Er hängt den Hörer wieder ein.

Gut, ich habe dafür gesorgt, dass Sie jemanden treffen können, der ein bisschen Licht in die Sache bringen könnte. Nehmen Sie das.
Er kritzelt eine Notiz auf ein Stück Papier und gibt es DER AUTORIN, die sich erhebt. Wenn Sie dies beim Empfang zeigen, wird man Ihnen alles Weitere sagen.
Sie geben.

AUSSEN. DIE GLASFAS-
SADE EINES GROSSEN
GEBÄUDES. EINE STADT.
TAG
Menschen betreten und verlassen das Gebäude durch eine Drehtür.

AUSSEN. EINE STRASSE
IN EINER REICHEN
WOHNGEGEND. EINE
STADT. TAG
Luftaufnahme von DER AUTORIN und ihrem BEGLEITER, die gemeinsam irgendwohin gehen. DIE AUTORIN trägt die in Plastik eingeschlagene Schachtel unter dem Arm.

AUSSEN. VOR EINER
GROSSEN, SCHWARZEN
EINGANGSTÜR. EINE
STADT. ABEND
DER BEGLEITER sieht auf einem Stück Papier nach und drückt einen Klingelknopf. Als

das Schloss hörbar aufschnappt, sieht DER BEGLEITER DIE AUTORIN an und öffnet die Tür.

INNEN. EINE STEINERNE
TREPPENFLUCHT.
EINE STADT. ABEND
DIE AUTORIN und ihr BEGLEITER steigen die Treppe hoch.

INNEN. IMPROVISIERTER
HÖRSAAL. ABEND
Die Tür des Raumes öffnet sich, und DIE AUTORIN und ihr BEGLEITER werden von einem etwas älteren Mann mit ergrauendem Haar und Schnurrbart begrüßt. Unter seinem Arm trägt er ein gefülltes Diakarussell. Der Raum ist ein großes Wohnzimmer mit schwacher, gelblicher Beleuchtung. Entlang der Wände stehen Bücherregale, und zwei Stühle sind vor einer wackeligen Projektionsleinwand aufgestellt.

DER GELEHRTE, *noch bevor DIE AUTORIN und ihr BEGLEITER etwas sagen können und ohne sich vorzustellen:* Willkommen, willkommen. Nehmen Sie bitte Platz. Die Dokumentation und die Ergebnisse erhielten wir vor gut einer Stunde. Ich glaube, ich bin mehr oder weniger im Bilde, was die Situation betrifft. Bevor wir richtig loslegen, bitte ich Sie darum, Nachsicht mit mir zu haben. Nehmen Sie Platz.

Er hält die zerknitterten Dokumente in seiner Faust und deutet mit ihnen in Richtung der beiden Stühle.

DER BEGLEITER, *sitzend:* Danke sehr.

DER GELEHRTE: Kann ich Ihnen etwas anbieten?
Vergeblich versucht er, vor dem Spiegel seinen Schnurrbart zu glätten.

DIE AUTORIN: Danke, nein.

DER GELEHRTE dunkelt das Licht ab und schaltet einen Diaprojektor ein. Nahaufnahme des sich drehenden Karussells und eines Diawechsels. Halbnahaufnahme DER AUTORIN und ihres BEGLEITERS mit direktem Blick in die Kamera – als wäre diese in der Position der Leinwand, auf der die Dias gezeigt werden. DER GELEHRTE steht hinter den beiden.

DER GELEHRTE: Sitzen Sie bequem? Lassen Sie uns beginnen.
Er klickt zum nächsten Dia.
Im wirklichen Leben folgen auf die Momente der Liebe Momente der Übersättigung und des Schlafs. Der aufrichtigen Gefühlsäußerung folgt zynisches Misstrauen. Wahrheit ist fragmentarisch, bestenfalls: Wir lieben und betrügen einander nicht gerade im selben Atemzug, aber doch in zwei

Atemzügen, die sehr dicht aufeinanderfolgen. Jedoch sollte die Tatsache, dass Leidenschaft quasi beiläufig aufscheint und dann in eine vertrautere Form von Gleichgültigkeit absinkt, nicht als Beweis für ihre Inkonsequenz betrachtet werden. Und dies ist die einzige Wahrheit, die das Drama für uns bereithält.

Während DER GELEHRTE spricht, sind verschiedene Bilder zu sehen. Es bleibt unklar, ob dies die Dias sind, die DER AUTORIN und ihrem BEGLEITER gezeigt werden, oder ob es sich um eine assoziative Filmmontage handelt.
a) *Eine skelettartige Figurine.*
b) *Ein einzelnes, leeres Martiniglas.*
c) *Ein aus einem Steinblock gemeißeltes Frauengesicht.*
d) *Schmutziges Geschirr, das sich neben vollen Aschenbechern stapelt.*
e) *Boxer im Sparring.*
f) *Wolken aus Papierschlangen in einer Konfettiparade.*

Ob wir es uns eingestehen oder nicht, wir werden alle von einem wahrlich furchtbaren Sinn für Unbeständigkeit getrieben. Ich habe auf Cocktailpartys immer ein besonders ausgeprägtes Gespür dafür gehabt, und vielleicht trinke ich die Martinis deshalb fast so schnell wie ich sie vom Tablett schnappen kann. Dieser Sinn liegt fiebernd in der Luft.

Abscheu vor Unaufrichtigkeit, vor *Bedeutungslosigkeit*, überlagert diese Angelegenheiten wie die Rauchwolke einer Zigarette und hektisches Geschwätz. Dieser Abscheu ist fast das einzige, das bei solchen Anlässen unausgesprochen bleibt. Alle gesellschaftlichen Abläufe innerhalb einer Gruppe von Menschen, die sich nicht ganz genau kennen, stehen unter diesem Schatten. Sie sind fast immer, auf unbewusste Weise, wie dieses letzte Mahl der Verurteilten: wo Steak oder Truthahn, was immer der Verlorene möchte, in seiner Zelle als spöttisch grausame Erinnerung an die Angebote der großen-bedeutenden-kleinen-vergänglichen Welt serviert wird …
Er macht eine Pause und hält seine Hand schwerfällig vor den Mund.

Das Publikum kann sich in wohliger Dämmerung zurücklehnen, um eine lichtdurchflutete Welt zu betrachten, in der Empfindungen und Handlungen eine Dimension und Erhabenheit haben, die sie gleichermaßen im echten Leben hätten, wenn nur der erschütternde Einbruch der Zeit davon ausgeschlossen bliebe.[1]

DIE AUTORIN und ihr BEGLEITER sitzen schweigend da, verwirrt. Ein erneuter von einem Klicken begleiteter Diawechsel. Nahaufnahme des in Licht getauchten Gesichts DES BEGLEITERS. DER

GELEHRTE scheint hochzufrieden zu sein und schlurft zu seinen umfangreichen Bücherregalen. Er kommt mit einem Armvoll ehrwürdig aussehender Bände zurück.

DER GELEHRTE: Genug fabuliert. Die hier sind dazu aufgelegt zu helfen. Entschuldigen Sie das Wortspiel.

DIE AUTORIN und ihr BEGLEITER stehen auf, und er drückt DEM BEGLEITER die Bücher in die Arme.

DER BEGLEITER *kleinlaut:* Danke.

DER GELEHRTE: Vielleicht ist es am besten, wenn Sie den anderen Ausgang benutzen.

Er führt sie zu einer anderen, kleineren Seitentür. Sie verlassen den Raum, und man sieht sie in die prächtige Galerie eines städtischen Museums eintreten. Das Museum ist eindeutig geschlossen, und die Lichter sind gelöscht. Gemälde hängen an den Wänden, was sie jedoch darstellen ist bei der schwachen Beleuchtung nicht sichtbar. Sie erscheinen schwarz, nur angedeutet. DIE AUTORIN und ihr BEGLEITER sehen sich im Mondlicht, das durch die hohen Fenster fällt, an. DER BEGLEITER atmet aus, lächelt voller Zweifel und fährt mit den Fingern durch seine Haare. DIE

AUTORIN lächelt und sieht ihn
an. Er beginnt zu laufen, und
sie folgt ihm lachend nach. Totale
von den beiden wie sie rennen.
Der Klang ihrer Schritte hallt
in den leeren Fluren wider.

  * Ende von Spule 1

(Übersetzung: Barbara Uppenkamp,
Ralf Weißleder)

1 Tennessee Williams,
 The Timeless World of A Play,
 Vorwort des Autoren zu
 The Rose Tattoo, 1951

Page 5
Untitled (Le trou)
2009
Inkjet print on paper, frame
30 × 35 cm

A simple intervention in a film still from Jacques Becker's *Le trou* (1959). The still photograph was extracted from the movie's production flow 50 years ago; here, by cutting out the sand, time stops again. The hole with its contradictory shades does not fit perfectly into the picture and becomes the focus of review. Whoever looks at it gets in mysterious complicity.

Page 42
Untitled
1999/2007
Two channel video projection
13:19 min

Untitled is based on the point-of-view shots from the central scenes in Michelangelo Antonioni's classic *Blowup* (1966). At this moment in the film, while making enlargements, the photographer protagonist detects a corpse in Maryon Park in London. Meyer eliminated all actors by retouching so that the double projection only depicts the park with the wind rustling in the trees. The digital masking and construction of a gap point to the question of cinematic reality, a theme raised in the original movie.

Page 51
Saved from Fire (1–3)
2007/2008
Books, wood
Variable sizes

François Truffaut's movie *Fahrenheit 451* (1966), adapted from the novel of the same title by Ray Bradbury, is the reference for the selection of books on the three bookshelf-objects *Saved from Fire*. Depicting a dystopian future where reading is outlawed each selection of books corresponds to their appearance in a scene of book burning. Here however they remain intact apparently preserved across space and time.

Page 61
À rebours
2008
Single channel video projection
34:43:50 hours

Matthias Meyer made his first film based only on the 1884 text by Joris-Karl Huysmans' *À rebours* (Against the Grain). One after another, every single letter of the novel appears in the centre of the screen. The complete book in its original French version is virtually spelled out, so that, after all, the text remains readable. Of course, the sheer duration of the projection exceeds the viewer's attentiveness. Slowness plays an important role in Huysmans' novel with, for example, the decadent, aristocratic protagonist Jean Des Esseintes loving nothing more than walking his turtle, adorned with jewels. The novel is a powerful, eloquent, introspective description of the artificial world of Des Esseintes, who constantly devises new kicks as an escape from the boredom of reality. In contrast to this, Meyer's video is a minimalist test assembly, where all cinematic means are negated to prioritise language. Reducing the atmosphere of the book to its single letters does not mean that the novel is vanishing, but rather it is transferred to a formal structure. Here the process of individual perception takes the place of clear information brokering. Matthias Meyer does not intend to dismantle cinematic syntax into its component elements nor does he try to evoke a greater entity by exposing singular semantic layers, which are only shaped fragmentarily with their cinematic or literary references. The process of decomposition creates works, which are based on clearly nameable structures, while nevertheless remaining cryptic.

Vanessa Joan Müller

Page 67
A Museum of Its Memory
2009
Print on baryta paper
13 × 18 cm
In *A Museum of Its Memory* Meyer leads Chris Marker's film *La jetée* (1962) back to its photographic origin. All 566 photographs that comprise the original movie are superimposed to create one single photographic layer with the opacity of each image corresponding to the duration of its appearance in the film.

Page 71
Endless Ocean
2009
Wood, piezo print
94 × 17 × 19 cm
A nautical chart, rolled and thus closed. All the lines of navigation, longitudes, latitudes, and coordinates of its sign system merge in the manner of a Möbius strip with no beginning and no end.

Page 73
No Empire
2006
Single channel video projection
60:00 min, loop
Andy Warhol's movie *Empire* without the Empire State Building. Nothing remains except dirt, dust, scratches and the night sky over New York City. Some exposure errors are also visible in the footage which has now lost its central character and original conceptual motive.

Page 105
Untitled
2007
Ink, pumping system
Diameter 60 cm
A whirlpool of black ink is hidden in a hollow in the ground, between the trees and bushes of a park.

Page 109
Ghost
2005
Single channel video
projection
8:00 min

Views of the deserted mansion of
Curzio Malaparte on the Isle of
Capri. The ramshackle condition
of the building, which the author
conceived as his self-portrait,
becomes the focal point of the
video … non plus d'histoire(s).

Page 117
The Whirl
2007
12" record, 1 track
9:54 min

Simultaneously a record, object and
audio piece, based on Edgar Allan
Poe's short story *A Descent into the
Maelstrom*, this work provides a narration of Poe's protagonist and various
objects as they spin a frantic whirlpool.
Here they fill the room as the sound of
spoken words repeated over and over
again, but varying in order, while the
black vinyl revolves on the turntable.

*the man … the boat … the trunk …
the timber … the barrel … the boat…*

Page 118
Beaufort
2004
Single channel video
projection
6:02 min

Beaufort is a collage of revised clips
taken from the Hollywood classics
Moby Dick (1956) and *Mutiny on
the Bounty* (1962). In Beaufort both
archetypical sailing vessels Pequod
and Bounty merge to become a
single ghost ship sailing the seas
without a crew.

Page 127
Folded Fog
2008
Piezo print on paper
400 × 300 cm

Matthias Meyer's complex works
circle around the basic structure, the
modules of mainstream cultural
narration and the mechanisms of its
production: the book, movie, concert,
vinyl record, text, word, letter, piano,
musical composition, single note.

Using an animation soft-
ware Meyer creates an image with
the illusion that the field of vision
is obscured by a haze of fog. This is
reproduced in the form of a folded
bill with the scale of a cinema poster
(*Folded Fog*, 2008).

This way he points to the
illusionist and economic mechanisms
of the dream factories and plays with
the projected wishes of their consu-
mers. By erasing the plot's essential
aspects from the pictures and by

removing the virtual story line, Meyer enables the viewer to see the exposed mechanisms of the production of narration, illusion and ›Desire‹.

Stefan Kalmár

Page 131
Index
2008
Autopiano
Audio analysis of the
Moonshine Sonata by Ludwig van Beethoven (1801)

In *Index* (2008), Beethoven's romantic *Moonlight Sonata* (1801) is run through from A to Z. An autopiano is pro-grammed to play every tone of the composition in sequence in ascending order. The most frequent tone is the one that remains at the end.

Page 133
Kissing a Cloud
2001
C print
43 × 35 cm

Page 135
The Black Museum
2006
Single channel video projection
4:52 min

The Black Museum is constructed from scenes extracted from Nicolas Philibert's documentary *La Ville Louvre* (1990). These depict glances behind the scenes of museum work

Paris-style. All the paintings that would appear in the movie have been completely blackened. The time-honoured museum thus becomes a suprematist masterwork, informed by the aesthetics of negation picking its potential from the absurdity of a countless number of black pictures. Conservation teams, curators, and other members of the staff handle each picture like a »window to the world«, though this window remains closed to the viewer.

Page 143
Caught Darkness
2005
C print
35 × 45 cm

Page 145
Happy Ends
2001
Installation
Prima Kunst, Kiel

A windowless exhibition space: across its longest side a dark, full-length curtain, through which the audience accesses the room. Facing them higher up at the wall, there is a small opening behind which is a second room, from which light shines in. The gallery space resembles a cinema with no projection or a gloomy cellar. Instead of a screening, the diffuse atmosphere itself is the event. Opening time is from 8 to 10 p.m. A black poster advertises the exhibition baring information, which is arranged like a subtitle on its surface. A picture on its reverse shows a view of an unknown city lit by a full moon. This is the only image in the exhibition.

Page 152
Double
2000
Performance
apexart, New York
A duplicate of the gallery's key was handed over to an actor from New York with the instruction to lose it somewhere in Manhattan. No documentation exists of this action either in the exhibition space or the world outside.

Page 155
How can you smile when you're deep in thought?
2009
20 piezo prints on paper
27,5 × 32 cm each
How can you smile when you're deep in thought? is the tonal analysis of a recorded conversation between Morton Feldman and John Cage. It plays back the sound of speech and the voices of both protagonists, while they discuss essential questions concerning artistic production and how they conceive their work as composers. The pictorial transformation of this discourse into a musical score is enhanced by its subsequent musical interpretation as a performance on a vibraphone that fills the room with its hollow, metallic sound.

Page 165
*The Rising Snow/
The Falling Stars*
2009
Hardcover book, 164 pages
19,2 × 28,5 cm
Reading *The Rising Snow/The Falling Stars* works in two ways, with regard to its content and to its form respectively. The two book covers, front and verso, provide different titles for shared content. Inside the book, digitally generated small particles are dancing, hovering, and fluttering over the pages in cinematic, single-image sequence. Distance or closeness are not accessible. The fleeting impression of snowflakes simultaneously become eternal constellations on a potential starry sky.

Page 175
Smoke Archive
2010
C prints (selection)
Variable sizes
The *Smoke Archive* is a collection of scenes from movies, in which smoke is depicted. It's an apparently chaotic compilation, that is composed in different ways on every occasion.

Page 191
*Empty Moon for
an Empty Room*
2005
Single channel video
projection, loop

The emptied set design from Georges
Meliès' film *A Trip to the Moon* (1902)
serves as the awkwardly jolting
coulisse to illuminate the empty
exhibition room.

Page 193
Snowwww
2006
Offset print
32 × 24,5 cm

The central motive from Michael
Snow's *Wavelength* (1967) as both
a multiple and a silent film still.

Page 197
Sherwood
(1st Season, Parts 1–5)
2010
Single channel video
projection
14:53 min

An expedition through the thicket
of the history of motion pictures: the
episodic video *Sherwood* proposes a
move into the rough terrain of myths
and legends. It carries us off into
the most diverse representations of
this legendary forest. The work is
arranged like an archive. It consists
of remastered shots from big screen
adaptations of Robin Hood.

MATTHIAS MEYER,
geboren 1972 in Hameln, studierte
Freie Kunst an der Muthesius Hoch-
schule Kiel und an der Akademie
der bildenden Künste in Wien. Seine
Arbeiten wurden in Einzel- und Grup-
penausstellungen gezeigt, u. a. im
Kunstverein für die Rheinlande und
Westfalen Düsseldorf, Kunstmuseum
Bonn, Kunstverein Hamburg, Martin-
Gropius-Bau Berlin, DeSingel Antwer-
pen, Castello di Rivoli Turin, Galerie
Eva Winkeler Frankfurt/Köln und
Konrad Fischer Galerie Düsseldorf.
Er erhielt Preise und Stipendien, u. a.
den Brockmann Preis der Stadt Kiel,
Arbeitsstipendium der Stadt Hamburg,
Reisestipendium Neue Kunst in
Hamburg und das Atelierstipendium
Cité Internationale des Arts Paris.
Er lebt in Hamburg.

KATHA SCHULTE,
geboren 1967 in Herten, Westfalen,
studierte Germanistik und Italianistik.
Sie lebt und arbeitet als Schriftstelle-
rin, Filmkritikerin und freie Lektorin
in Hamburg. Im Oktober 2010 erschien
ihr Roman *Unwesen* im Hablizel Verlag.

KATHA SCHULTE,
born in Herten/Westphalia in 1967,
studied German and Italian Philology.
She lives in Hamburg where she works as
a writer, film critic and freelance reader.
In October 2010 the Hablizel Verlag
published her novel »Unwesen«.

MATTHIAS MEYER,
born in Hamelin in 1972, studied at the
Muthesius Academy of Fine Arts and Design
in Kiel, and at the Academy of Fine Arts in
Vienna. His work was displayed in several
institutions, including the Kunstverein für
die Rheinlande und Westfalen Düsseldorf,
Kunstmuseum Bonn, the Kunstverein
Hamburg, the Martin-Gropius-Bau Berlin,
the DeSingel Antwerp, the Castello di
Rivoli Turin, the Galerie Eva Winkeler
Frankfurt/Cologne and the Konrad Fischer
Galerie Düsseldorf. He received awards
and grants: the Brockmann Preis of the City
of Kiel, an artist's grant from the City of
Hamburg, a traveling scholarship donated
by Neue Kunst in Hamburg, and he was
artist in residence at the Cité Internationale
des Arts Paris. He lives in Hamburg.

GILES BAILEY
ist Künstler, geboren 1981 in York.
Er studierte in Glasgow und London
und zurzeit in Rotterdam. Sein Projekt
Talker Catalogue ist eine Montage
einer subjektiven Geschichte der Performance, bestehend aus gedruckten
Publikationen, fiktiven Geschichten
und Livestücken für Radio und Bühne.

GILES BAILEY
is an artist born 1981 in York. He studied
in Glasgow, London and now in Rotterdam
where he lives. Through his project »Talker
Catalogue« he is assembling a subjective
history of performance which includes prin-
ted publications, works of fiction in addition
to live pieces for the radio and stage.

Matthias Meyer
A NOBLE VOID

ISBN: 978-3-941613-38-6

Texte/Texts:
Katha Schulte, Giles Bailey

Übersetzungen/Translations:
Alice Bayandin, Barbara Uppenkamp, Ralf Weißleder

Lektorat/Proof Reading:
Gustav Mechlenburg, Ralf Weißleder

Gestaltung/Design:
Anna Sophie Bertermann, Hamburg

Fotos/Photographs:
Fred Dott: S./pg. 51, 59, 128–131, Wolfgang Günzel: S./pg. 61–71, 160–163,
Yun Lee: S./pg. 42–43, Thies Rätzke: S./pg. 52–57, 127, Matthias Meyer

Druck & Herstellung/Printed & Produced:
Vier-Türme GmbH – Benedict Press, Münsterschwarzach

*Mit bestem Dank für die Unterstützung bei der Produktion des vorliegenden Buches /
Heartfelt thanks for the support during the realisation of this book go to:*
Giles Bailey, Alice Bayandin, Anna Bertermann, Hagen Bertermann,
Julien Diehn, Ingo Gerken, Stefan Kalmár, Christoph Laucht, Linda McCue,
Gustav Mechlenburg, Renate und Jürgen Meyer, Vanessa Joan Müller,
Katha Schulte, Nora Sdun, Barbara Uppenkamp, Ralf Weißleder, Eva Winkeler

Printed in Germany
Auflage: 600

Textem Verlag
www.textem-verlag.de

Diese Publikation wurde gefördert durch die/This publication was supported by:
Behörde für Kultur und Medien der Freien und Hansestadt Hamburg